TRUE
WEST

David Whish-Wilson was born in Newcastle, NSW, but grew up in Singapore, Victoria and Western Australia. He left Australia at eighteen to live for a decade in Europe, Africa and Asia. He is the author of *The Summons*, *The Coves* and *The Sawdust House*, and four crime novels in the Frank Swann series: *Line of Sight*, *Zero at the Bone*, *Old Scores* and *Shore Leave*. *True West* (featuring Lee Southern) was shortlisted for a Ned Kelly Award for Best Crime. Its sequel, *I Am Already Dead*, also features Lee Southern. His non-fiction book, *Perth*, part of the NewSouth Books City series, was shortlisted for a WA Premier's Book Award, and in 2022 David was shortlisted for a Western Australian Writer's Fellowship. David lives in Fremantle and coordinates the creative writing program at Curtin University.

TRUE WEST

DAVID WHISH-WILSON

 FREMANTLE PRESS

For Andrew

PART I

WESTERN AUSTRALIA, 1988

1.

Lee Southern drove with his palm against the steering wheel. He liked to feel the machinery blow in its tight iron constellation while he held the picture in his mind. The Ford F350 felt like an extension of his body and like him it was seventeen years old. Lee's father had bought it on the day that Lee was born. The minute he heard that Lee's mother was in labour he drove to the Geraldton Ford dealership and bought the F350 utility with its 351 Cleveland engine and straight green paint job.

Lee rested his arm on the driver's sill and let his hand wobble in the wind. The sun was headed toward the horizon and he could smell the baked limestone crests that rose and fell alongside him like the flanks of a snake. The floor of the tuart and banksia scrublands was covered in purple, blue, pink, white and yellow wildflowers. Spring was his favourite season but he wasn't looking at the flowers today.

Lee glanced in his wing mirror like he'd been doing the last five hours. They would be coming for him if they weren't already. Some of them on bikes, some of them in their tricked-up Landy 4WDs.

The Knights would be coming as soon as they discovered their latest five-acre plantation had been destroyed: cropped to the base of the stalk and raked into mounds and set on fire with diesel.

Lee still had ash and dirt and the smell of mary-jane smoke on his hands, jeans and t-shirt. He'd left the acreage before dawn with the orange flames pumping flak-gun smuts into the bluing sky.

Lee patted the dash of the truck and eased on the accelerator. Just thinking about what he'd done made him speed. The Knights would be looking for his father's Holden Sandman, with its swirling death's-head decals along the sides and its *Knights01* plates – bestowed upon Jack Southern as first president of the club. Now that Lee's father was missing, Lee'd been ordered to return the plates to Greg Downs, the new Knights president and probable killer of his father. Instead, Lee had gone and torched their plantation.

Lee put his hand on the wheel and felt the tappets beating their quiet rhythm and the pistons firing and all of it a controlled dance of fire and fuel. The Ford F350 truck had been parked under a tarp at his uncle Gary's block outside Dongara. It was unlicensed and untraceable – the perfect vehicle for him to escape in.

Lee reached for the dash and took out a cigarette. The truck kept on straight without his hands on the wheel because of all the weight. It was fitted out to provide him with an income when he got to the city. Last week, Lee and his uncle Gary had cut off the ute-bed and replaced it with an iron sheet. There were blocks of pig-iron ballast in the engine bay to balance out the home-crafted towing rig they'd bolted to the iron sheet. Onto that, Lee and his uncle had welded a winch scavenged from a Mack truck. A steel box filled with dollies and canvas slings and stands, chocks and jacks. A diesel generator and air compressor. Air cushions taken from his father's fifty-foot trawler. Snatch blocks and spare chain. Heavy-duty rope and steel cable. Bridles and skates and arrow sticks. A shovel and broom and tarpaulin. A toolbox and first-aid kit.

There was a whine that became a throaty roar and Lee took the wheel and stared in the wing mirror until he saw the riders. He was rolling at one hundred but they were coming on him – two riders in black leathers floating through the silver heat mirage and leaning into the banking turn. Lee reached under the seat for his father's Luger pistol. Before his father owned it, his grandfather had ratted it from a German officer in North Africa. His grandfather had pointed it at the German officer and, because they were instructed not to take prisoners, had tested it on the officer's brainpan. The pistol was Lee's father's favourite. He brandished it at meetings and fired it down at the gun club and disassembled and cleaned it whenever he needed to think.

Lee drove one-handed with the pistol aimed at his feet and looked back at the riders who'd moved out of single file and were now in tandem. He flicked off the safety and fingered the magazine that was supposed to hold eight rounds but because of the tight spring only held seven. The riders were signalling to one another. Lee's instinct was to speed but the truck was top-heavy and cornered badly. He eased his foot and slowed to eighty, and then seventy, and held the pistol and calmed his breathing. The Luger was semiautomatic and if he wasn't careful he'd shoot out the magazine in seconds, and then he'd be unarmed.

The road dipped into the crazed pastel colours of the coastal woodland. The only movement ahead was a raven swimming in the watery mirage with roadkill in its beak. Lee could see the city as a brown smudge on the southern horizon, and then the bikes were alongside him, and then they were ahead, and he didn't recognise the twin BMWs or the riders whose panniers were full of camping supplies. They were soon out of sight and Lee immobilised the pistol and slipped it under his seat.

To steady himself, he checked the gauges and dials. Temperature and oil pressure were fine. His speed was regular. Another kilometre clicked over on the trip meter – three hundred so far. The fuel gauge was the only problem, headed toward empty. The V8 engine was thirsty and he only had forty-five dollars in his pocket. The plan was to hit the freeways as soon as he got to the city and hopefully snag a tow.

The rig rattled and the suspension creaked and the sun was warm on his arm. He liked the colour of his skin when it got a belting of sun. The regular creamy chocolate-milk colour went a deep iodine red. It was the same colour as his father's skin that was year-round reddish-brown like the dirt in their yard and which made the black of his father's hair and the blue of his eyes more startling real.

Lee began to pass cars coming the other way, overtaking the long-haul road trains headed to the Pilbara mine sites laden with WABCO tyres, dongas, fleet vehicles and water tanks.

The brown bomber he'd taken before setting the plantation alight was wearing off – the first waves of fatigue and nausea began to tremble through his body. He hadn't eaten for thirty-six hours. He had thirteen bombers left but wanted to save them – the last of his father's stash. His father often went a week without sleep. He was fine for the first few days until he began shooting the speed every hour, and then his head went sideways and his paranoia grew. Lee would get the guns together and hide them in the shed, except for the Luger, which never left his father's belt.

There were pine plantations now. Lee wiped his eyes and then there were strawberry farms, plots growing cabbage and lettuce, and he could see the conical hats of Vietnamese in the fields. He tuned the radio and found a university station that was playing a Beasts of Bourbon track. Lee's music was in the trunk out back – Saxon, Slayer, Anthrax, Black Sabbath, AC/DC, Metallica, the new Megadeth, a whole lot of mixtapes.

The only music in the deck was one of his father's Johnny Cash compilations, bought at a Paynes Find service station when Lee was eleven and they were returning from one of their missions: leaving caches of weapons and food in the desert for when the invasion came. The Beasts of Bourbon track ended and now it was a new band called Guns N' Roses, and Lee tapped along, and then he saw the Volvo pulled into a cutaway with its bonnet up. Lee slowed the rig and pulled onto the hard shoulder, rolled into the graded dirt behind the car.

She was sitting on a red pudding rock in the sparse shade of an old tuart, smoking a cigarette and looking at a road map. The woman put the map down and followed him with her eyes. Lee climbed from the truck and hitched his jeans and ran a hand over his cropped head. Her expression didn't change as she tapped ash onto the dirt, and it was only her eyes that were smiling. She was about twice his age. Her skin was pale and she wore tight jeans and leather boots. She didn't get up – just flicked glossy hair off her face and waved at a fly.

'That truck. Those jeans. That smudged t-shirt. Your face. You look like a Calvin Klein advertisement.'

Lee didn't know what that meant but he smiled, because she was smiling now, reaching out a hand for him to lift her up. She weighed hardly anything at all.

She dug her heels in the bauxite gravel and stepped in a careful fashion toward the Volvo, as though she wasn't used to walking on anything but carpet and cut grass.

'Something went bang, and then everything seized up, and I glided in neutral until I found this spot.'

'Is anyone coming for you?'

The question seemed to concern her, and she bit her lip and looked at her hands then stared him in the eye. 'I was going to flag down a police car. They come down the road quite regularly.'

She wasn't from around here, and couldn't know the police routines, but he understood and nodded toward the car. 'You want me to take a look?'

He knew as soon as the words left his mouth that it was the wrong move, offering to fix her car when he had a perfectly good towing rig right there. Then he remembered her description of the engine going bang, and that could only mean one thing – good news for him and bad luck for her.

Lee touched the inside of the bonnet that was cold under his fingers. The engine was cold too, meaning she'd been there some hours. He leaned over the driver's seat and turned the key. The engine wouldn't crank. He dropped the bonnet and wiped his hands on his shirt. 'Was she running a bit off before the bang?'

'Yes, like a three-legged horse.'

'First you blew a head gasket, and then you lost water and overheated, and then you threw a piston into the cylinder head. That was the bang. I'm sorry to say this, lady, but your engine's finished. I can tow –'

'Please. That'd be marvellous. Will you take a cheque?'

Lee struggled for the right answer. He wanted to say yes, but a cheque was no good. He didn't have a bank account and didn't know how to cash a cheque. It was part of his father's ethos to avoid banks unless you were robbing them.

'How about you fill up my truck at the next servo, and some of the jerry cans, and we'll take it from there.'

He expected her to look worried at his answer, exposing his operation as half-arsed, but she smiled and put out her hand

and Lee wiped his hand on his jeans and they shook on it.

'I ride with you?'

He realised he was staring at her and broke off the handshake and nodded. 'Go back into the shade until I've put her in the sling. Won't be long.'

Lee turned toward his truck. His uncle Gary had shown him how to hitch a car but he'd never done it himself. The Volvo was a rear-wheel drive and he'd have to sling it to the back axle. He headed for the steel box and made a picture of everything he'd need, which in this case was only a canvas sling. He lit a cigarette as he walked and took out a brown bomber from his pocket and swallowed it. He would be making conversation for the next hour at least, and needed the spur-on. Lee wished the woman wasn't so friendly with him – he needed to concentrate on the road, and then get to where the paying work was.

2.

The woman's name was Sophia and he liked her better with every passing minute. She had a throaty voice that deepened when she chuckled, which was often. Their conversation took his mind off what he had done and what he was running from. She sat on the bench seat and touched his arm to make her points. Even though she was thirty-six years old, the same age his mother would've been, she didn't flirt like the leery women his father drank with at the Tarcoola Tavern. Lee had been with plenty of girls, but they were just that – girls – with the exception of Emma, and he didn't want to think about her.

There was an awkward few minutes when Sophia tried to draw him out. She wanted to know about his mother and father and where he was from. Lee stiffened in his seat and his arms went rigid on the wheel – his father's voice in his head. *This woman is an outsider.*

There was a time a few years ago when Lee started the day with a bucket bong, just to get through it all. The bush weed came from their plantations and it was strong and clean but it began to turn him weird. He started to suspect that his schoolteachers were federal police, sent to observe him. He'd once topped every class, but he stopped handing his homework in. It wasn't until one of their plantation-sitters cleaved open his friend's skull with an axe, just because he'd begun to suspect his friend was a spy, that Lee realised the effect the bud was having. It was the family business, all for the cause, but he stopped smoking that day and had never gone back to it. Getting paranoid-weird wasn't dangerous for some citizens, he supposed, but for his father's people, who were all trained in violence, the consequences were lethal.

Lee put the thoughts of Geraldton out of his head. He tried instead to enjoy the sound of Sophia's voice and the blood that was pumping through his limbs in a syncopated rhythm and the way his skin hummed because of the brown bomber kicking in. He drank from a carton of iced coffee and waited for her to finish her hamburger, which had covered the wrapper in her lap with shreds of beetroot, carrot and lettuce. Her can of Passiona sat in the cup holder, untouched since she'd tasted it that first time. The tank was full of petrol and the reserve tank and jerries were full and the woman was pretty entertaining, telling him about her ex-boyfriend, who was some kind of lawyer from a rich family. How she'd found photographs of him in a shoebox in their walk-in closet. He was facedown in all of the photographs, with his hands and feet bound to bedposts, and there were switch marks on his back. In one photo he had a broom handle up his arse. The photographs didn't worry her as much as you might think, she said, it was more his reaction when she laid them on their bed. He flat out denied it was him in the photographs. He denied it even after Sophia said that it didn't matter, because it was a turn-on to see a man explore the boundaries of his need, and that she wouldn't mind exploring them with him. But he kept denying it and then he started to get angry and finally he told her to leave. It was *over*, he said, and if she ever mentioned the photographs he'd cut her throat. All in less than a minute. Her chuckle at the absurdity of his reaction. The coward. Who'd vowed to spend the rest of his life with her, but who didn't want her to see him as anything other than the sailing club stalwart and legal rising star that she'd known since her teens.

She didn't regret the break-up, except for the fact that he'd taken back their Mercedes. But what could she do? He was a lawyer with deep pockets who could sue her.

Which gave Lee an idea; the speed coming on strongly now, making him want to impress her, making him want to do *something* to staunch the nerves in his belly.

They were in the city's northern suburbs, headed down Wanneroo Road where the banksia scrub had given way to a horizon packed with orange terracotta roofs.

'Take the coast road,' she said, 'there's less traffic.'

Lee panicked for a moment. He hadn't been to the city for many years and didn't know his way around. He didn't want to call attention to the fact that his sole compass was the knowledge that if he kept to Wanneroo Road then he'd end up in the city centre, and from there he'd be able to see the freeway.

So he answered, casual as he could, 'Where does your ex live?'

He could feel her looking at him. 'Take the next right, over toward North Beach. He lives in City Beach.'

Lee decided to come clean. 'I don't know where I'm going, so you'll have to guide me there.'

She laughed. 'I thought so. At first I assumed you were returning from the city – I noticed your city plates, but you're giving off a different vibe.'

The city plates on the truck were stolen from a tourist van outside the Tarcoola a month ago, and he wondered if she wondered. 'What kind of vibe?'

'Like a refugee from a Tom Waits song.'

He glanced at her and put his eyes back on the road. He didn't know what the hell she was talking about, but she didn't let him wonder too long. 'So you don't have a phone number people can call you on when they get stuck?'

He shook his head. The traffic had begun to thicken as workers returned from the city.

'No phone number, no map, how are you going to get customers?'

All Lee had was a memory that'd stayed with him since he was a child, visiting the city while his father did a shady deal with an elderly man in a suburb called Kenwick. They were supposed to head back to Geraldton, but his cashed-up father suggested that they divert to Fremantle to get some Cicerello's fish and chips. On a hard shoulder off the Kwinana Freeway was a tow truck – a Bedford with a homemade rig. The driver was seated on the roobar, smoking a cigarette and reading a newspaper, oblivious to the traffic that hurtled alongside. It was only a moment but it stayed with Lee, and last week when he knew that he was city-bound, the image crystallised into something more real.

'You'll need this at the very least.'

She put the UBD street directory on the seat between them, tapped ash into the Passiona can. The road lifted over a crest and suddenly there was the Indian Ocean, vivid blue and silvered with southerly chop. Lee had just travelled three hundred and fifty K, but this was the same ocean that pounded the shoreline behind the dunes where he lived with his father – the bush block strewn with cannibalised car bodies and guard dogs that hunted rabbits in the scrub at night. The sight of the ocean made him feel at home.

'Beautiful, isn't it?'

She was looking at his unguarded expression of relief. He grunted and wiped his eyes, felt his shoulders loosen, realised he'd been propped forward like a worried child.

'We're on the coast road now, which leads to Fremantle. Until they build the freeway north, use this or Wanneroo Road to get up here. You really don't know your way around the city? Where are you planning to stay?'

Lee didn't like the question, and he didn't answer it. The ocean was replaced by grassed verges, power poles and peppermint trees. The light was soft and buttery, and the air was cooling fast. They rolled through a lowland park that was green and damp and was probably once a swamp. Say what you wanted about Lee's father – Jack Southern knew the land. He'd always schooled Lee on what the environment had been like, even in the city, which he considered a malignant growth. When the invasion came, it'd be the country that'd sustain the renegades, and they'd better learn to feed off her, and feed her back.

'Not far now.'

They were alongside the ocean again, and there were the familiar sand dunes and coastal heath, shrouded in pink and purple light.

'This is City Beach, and up on the hill's my ex's place. Hard to see because of the glare, but it's that white box on the corner with the ocean view.'

Lee couldn't see any house, just a big white block with tinted windows facing west. Didn't even have a roof on it, or a garden, or even a fence. Like Sophia said, a big white box.

The truck laboured up the dual carriageway that carried traffic from the beach, and Lee listened to the engine under strain like he had a stethoscope in his ears. It all sounded good, and he took the cigarette that Sophia offered as she lit one for herself. It was hard to read whether the expression on her face was excitement or anxiety, but either way she pointed him left, then left again. There was nobody on the street and each of the houses had high walls. They drove past the white box. Apart from a potted palm on the drive the front was bleak and anonymous. The rendered white wall was double his height and the garage had a white roller door.

Lee scoped the street for dog-walkers, but it was empty.

Every house had security cameras, however, trained on the drive and the yard.

'Not real inconspicuous, this truck, is it?' she said.

Lee agreed. He pulled around the corner where there were no cameras and got out. His number plates were hinged, as his father had taught him. He covered the plates on Sophia's car with rags and lifted up his own, got back in the truck and reversed around the corner and down onto the drive.

He looked at her. 'You sure?'

The barest nod of her head.

'He have an alarm system?'

'Yes, but he never turns it on. Don't think he even remembers the numbers.'

Lee passed his cap and indicated that she pull it low. He took a crowbar and a slim jim from the toolbox and levered the crowbar under the left side of the roller door and cracked the steel bracket, then did the same on the other side. He lifted the roller door and waited for an alarm. A car passed on the street but he didn't turn his head. The little black Mercedes was parked alongside a Porsche 928. He got the slim jim down inside the Mercedes driver's window and lifted the lock. He used the crowbar to shank off the steering cowling. He found the ignition wiring and pulled it out of the key-turn, joined the wires and turned the engine over.

Barely thirty seconds had passed. He climbed into the truck's cab and Sophia climbed out. No words were spoken, which impressed him. Like she'd done this before.

Lee put the Ford into gear and rolled up out of the drive,

and then he heard the breaking glass. She was smashing up the Porsche, which didn't impress him. But he was on his way. Seconds later, she overtook him on the corner and smiled and waved and settled in front. Every now and then she accelerated ahead but always fell back. The truck was sluggish under load and he didn't remember Perth being so hilly. This was limestone country, made of ancient sand dunes hardened over time. Drill down into it, his father had told him, and there was a freshwater sea. The thought of his father and the adrenalin that was dumping from his bloodstream were balanced out by the amphetamine that kept Lee's head clear and made his body shiver.

Sophia was taking rat-runs down leafy streets. He lit a cigarette and wiped his eyes. When they crested a final hill he couldn't believe the size of the place. There was the city shimmering in the distance. All around it were suburbs as far as he could see. A faint smog settled over the great sand plain, and the range to the east was burnt looking, and beat down. They were some of the oldest rocks in the world. The range had once been mountains but for billions of years of abrading heat and rain. The grids of houses on the sand plain looked as permanent as tents.

*

It was dark by the time they reached Sophia's home in Mosman Park. Stirling Highway was busy with traffic, and the streetlights made his eyes sting. Most of all he wanted to stay with his plan of doing a complete run of the Kwinana Freeway, to find a place to park up and wait. Lee didn't have the petrol to cruise the roads and needed a position where he could see if someone was broken down and needing help.

Lee parked beside a gnarled old peppermint tree and Sophia rapped on the window. He nodded to her and climbed out of the truck. The air smelled of resin on account of the Norfolk Island pines that rose above the homes up and down the hill. They were still in limestone country, and he could smell the briny ocean, or perhaps the river. This was clearly a rich area. Most of the houses were two-storey brick buildings with balconies and tin roofs. There were some blocks of flats in the distance that looked like termite mounds.

Sophia was talking to him but the sound came from a great distance. Lee nodded and pulled the winch lever and lowered the Volvo to the ground. He got on his knees in the dust and unhooked the canvas sling and pulled it loose. He stowed it in the steel box and fixed the padlock. He stood back and rubbed his eyes, felt himself shifting in the sea breeze.

'Look at you. You're so tired you're wobbling. I won't take no for an answer. At least take a cold shower and wake yourself up.'

The Mercedes engine ticked as it cooled. He could smell the sour oil that leaked from its belly.

'You need to change the oil in the Merc,' he said.

She laughed. 'That can wait.'

He let her take his elbow. They walked arm in arm down the drive, arched over with some kind of vine. It was an oddly formal way of walking but Lee didn't mind. He could feel the heat of her skin in the press of her elbow against his forearm. She released him at the porch of her weatherboard home when a security light came on. Moths began to circle the light. Then she had his elbow again, and he was in a long hallway with cool dark floorboards. The place smelled of jasmine and everything was white. She flicked switches as they entered deeper into the house. The backyard was full of flowering bottlebrushes that had dropped red bristles onto the bricked patio. The kettle began to hiss, and then it stopped hissing, and instead a fridge opened and he watched Sophia pull the cork from a bottle of white. She poured two glasses then passed him one. The wine tasted cold and sweet and he drank it down. That made her smile, and she led him to the bathroom that was all yellow tiles with prints of cockatoos and native flowers. There were towels and bras hanging out of a washing basket. The room smelled of coconut. The shower began to run and then he was alone. He stripped down and walked into the jet of hot water. He leaned his head on the tiles and let the water bash his shoulders, watching the cinders and dirt eddy at his feet as the stink of the fire was washed from his body.

3.

Lee Southern was used to waking to a dawn chorus of wattlebirds, honeyeaters and magpies in the saltbush scrub behind their Geraldton home. Last night he'd slept on the couch, and the alien rumble of traffic on Stirling Highway and Sophia's hesitant snoring in the nearby bedroom were loud enough that he couldn't return to sleep. He lay there until sunlight framed the heavy drape curtains that took up the eastern wall of the lounge. He had no idea what time it was, and barely remembered last night.

He didn't want to wake her. On the floor beside the couch were his clothes, folded beside his boots. On top of his clothes were his truck keys, inside the cap he'd told her to wear.

Lee stood and picked up the bundle, then began to dress. The sunlight was fierce in the kitchen and he drank four glasses of water and left by the front door.

*

The traffic into the city was steady until the suburbs broke and the Swan River opened wide and tea-coloured. The two-lane was snug against the Kings Park cliff face that was covered with the purple flowers of Geraldton wax and the orange fruits of zamia palm. The abandoned Swan Brewery to his right looked like a haunted castle. There were some derelicts sitting in the sun beside the brewery, their naked feet poised above the river.

Now that he was near the freeway, Lee turned on the UHF radio that his father had installed in the truck. It was important for a man who carried contraband to know the police frequencies in every city and town. In Perth, the coppers broadcast between 467MHz and 469MHz. The UHF didn't have the range of CB but the sound was clearer, and there were no problems with powerline interference. The sweet spot was 468.8, and there was a crackle and then a communication in code that Lee didn't understand. The code that Lee needed to identify was the one for a traffic accident. It would also pay to learn which traffic cops went by which signal number; a friendly or helpful cop especially. Cops he discovered to be unfriendly he could just avoid.

The morning traffic was snarled at the interchange that forked onto the Narrows Bridge. Most of the traffic turned left into the city, but Lee kept straight over the roundabout and then he was banking into a turn that brought him round onto the bridge and south over the river. His eyes were drawn to the pelicans and shags on the water, but he focused instead on the traffic, looking for a place to park the truck. This was the busiest route into the city and the lanes were bumper-

to-bumper, right down to Canning Highway. He didn't know
if this was the result of an accident, or was normal for peak
hour, but any situation where you get tens of thousands
of cars together in one place, there was always going to be
breakdowns and accidents. He just needed to find the place
to wait.

The traffic was lighter heading away from the city. Lee
slowed into the emergency lane to test the width of his truck
against the traffic breaking past. The sign said no stopping,
and he rejoined the flow of traffic and kept to the slow lane,
watching the frustrated looks on the faces of those headed
north. He looked for a stalled vehicle that might explain the
jam. Pretty soon he was near Canning Highway, and he took
the exit and turned onto Canning Bridge. He searched for
the apron he'd seen that other tow truck parked upon those
many years ago. But it wasn't there. Perhaps the road had been
widened, or perhaps he was on the wrong road, Lee didn't
know. He had no choice but to cross the bridge and search on
the other side. He found a side street a kilometre to the east.
It was the first side street that wasn't blanked with concrete
barriers. Lee pulled up behind a parked Mitsubishi van and
killed the engine. He kept the radio on and went and pissed
against a tree. He returned to the cab, lit a cigarette and felt
the heat building on the steel above his head. He reached for
the UBD street directory and began to memorise it, starting
by locating where he was parked. He read the names of the
major streets that radiated out from the freeway.

The radio crackled and went silent, and then burst with

static. 'Charlie 44. Civilian just called in a minor accident on corner of Scott Street and Mill Point Road. White Pajero disabled across one lane. VW Beetle pushed onto median strip. Please respond.'

The radio hissed in reply but Lee wasn't listening. He'd been looking at the South Perth map where the streets fed onto the freeway lanes north and south. Mill Point Road wasn't far from where he was parked. He closed the UBD and laid it on the seat beside. If he headed toward the river, he'd see the accident. He turned the key and pulled from the kerb, making good time until he reached Mill Point Road, where beneath the apartment towers his lane became blocked. Lee put the gear into neutral and opened the door and stood on his seat. He looked over the stalled traffic but there were no flashing blue lights. He got seated again and indicated into the oncoming lane. There were two hundred metres to cover. He wished he had an orange light on his roof to encourage the traffic headed his way to pull over until he passed. He drove down the middle of the road, two wheels on the concrete median strip while flashing his headlights. The tow rig was higher than his cab and anyone with half a brain could see it, but there was still confusion, and some idiot sat on his horn shaking his fist until Lee passed him, swinging round the crash site. He pulled in front of the white Pajero.

First on the scene. No coppers yet either. The driver of the Pajero was a man in a suit, seated behind the wheel. The front end of the 4WD was crushed in. He held a hankie against his forehead. The Beetle was already angled toward the kerb. The driver was a young woman in a tracksuit who stood under a nearby peppermint tree smoking a cigarette. Lee nodded at the VW, whose rear section was smashed, and she nodded back. He got down on his knees and saw that the undercarriage was intact and he put his head in the open window and took it out of gear. He got behind the door and with one hand put some weight behind the steering. He pushed the car across the lane onto the grass verge.

Lee went over to the Pajero driver. 'You'll have to get out, mate.'

The driver didn't respond, but when Lee opened the door he climbed out anyway, holding his head and taking his brief-case. He joined the woman in the shade.

Lee put the 4WD out of gear and ran to his truck and did a quick three-point turn and backed up. It was a straight sling tow, and he took out the canvas and got down on his knees. He attached the slings and then went to the winch and released some chain. He hooked the slings and took up the slack, then winch-lifted the Pajero's rear wheels. There was a side street twenty metres away. He got into the cab and put her in gear. He felt the weight and hoped that the front-end ballast was sufficient. He edged the truck forward until he was sure, and then eased down on the accelerator. He took the corner and parked in front of a dark-windowed law firm, killed the engine then took a broom and went back around the corner. The traffic had started to edge around the broken glass and chunks of the Beetle's tail-lights. He walked out into the traffic and put up a hand and began sweeping glass to the kerb. Then the traffic began to flow. He leaned on the broom and watched it pass.

The whole rescue took less than three minutes. He reached into his pocket to retrieve his pencil stub and drew out four crisp notes. Sophia had stashed two hundred dollars in his pocket. She must've gone out while he was asleep.

Lee went to the pair involved in the accident. There were still no coppers on the scene. The woman offered him a cigarette, a menthol, which he accepted. The man took away the hankie and the small gash on his forehead started to ooze blood.

'It was my fault,' the young woman said. 'I put on my indicator too late.'

Some rapport between the two. She put the man's hankie back onto his head. 'I'm a surgery nurse. That's going to be fine. No stitches, but keep the pressure on.'

Lee took out the notebook from his back pocket and flipped it open to the first page, the pencil poised.

He glanced up and there was another tow truck, pulling alongside to get a look at him. It was a white Mercedes rig. True West Towing decal above a custom-painted Australian flag. The tow driver wasn't much older than Lee, but solid and tattooed. Wore a white collared shirt buttoned to the top. Pale skin and a wide face that was giving Lee fish-eyes. Beside him was another man, and a young woman who was looking straight ahead. She had short black asymmetrical hair and bare arms.

The driver slung an arm out the window and put his head out, slowed to a crawl. Seemed about to say something when they heard the police siren, coming off the freeway north. The tow-truck driver smiled and turned to the wheel, then moved down the road.

*

Lee was paid sixty dollars to tow the Pajero to a panelbeaters on Manning Road, not far from the freeway. He returned and towed the Beetle to the same place, after the man in the suit recommended it to the young woman. He'd paid for her tow, and they caught a taxi together into the CBD.

Lee filled up the Ford at a Canning Highway service station, which ate up twenty dollars. His father had fitted the truck with long-range tanks in the late '70s when he was certain that war was coming. The truck could cover five hundred kilometres of off-road terrain before it needed refilling. Lee's dad also kept a couple of full jerries in the tray, too, and a locked steel box that contained a shotgun, some pineapple grenades and rations to last a week. They'd buried enough rations and weaponry out in the bush to last a year of guerrilla warfare. Jack Southern believed that once the invasion came and the cities fell, it'd be the Knights and others like them who'd prevail. They trained for survival, and there was no ideology beyond surviving the coming invasion. The shotgun was loaded with twelve-gauge pig-shot cartridges, sufficient to blast their way through any kind of conflict situation. Those cartridges were his father's favourites, because he'd used them in Vietnam. They weren't 3 RAR standard issue but he'd won the shotgun and a box of cartridges from an American in an arm-wrestle, and used them in the stony hills outside Nui Dat to flush out Vietcong insurgents. One blast, his father said, could disappear a man from his boots to his hat.

How Lee's dad got the shotgun and pineapple grenades back into Australia was never mentioned, although whenever Lee was frightened as a child – afraid of fighting at school, or of diving with sharks, or training with knives and live ammunition – his punishment was to sleep for a week with a live grenade under his pillow. The pins were bent backwards to make it hard to pull, but Lee didn't know that, and he didn't sleep well the first couple of nights. Sometimes his hand would touch the cold iron surface, and once he even awoke with his hand around the grenade like he was clutching a softball. But by the end of the week he was used to it, and then his father would lead him outside into the dunes and pull the pin and toss the grenade into a swale. They'd lie against the cold drift until the grenade detonated and covered them with sand.

*

The sun was heating up, and the air smelled of flowers and cut grass from all the people who'd watered their yards before heading off to work. Lee was parked in the side street off Canning Highway listening to the UHF, but was finding it hard to focus. He was pretty certain that the thoughts of his father were insistent because the Knights were coming for him, and he needed to be sharp. They were probably out there now in the desert camps, looking for him. They wouldn't figure on his heading for the city, but there was no way to be sure. Burning the plantation was something he'd started to regret, but in the end, it didn't matter. They'd killed his father and wanted to kill him too. Lee knew all their operational matters. He was gone from the fold.

The smoke from his cigarette drifted out of the cab. There was a chitty-chitty scratching about on the truck's bonnet, stropping its beak on the duco before launching up to snatch a moth that it brought back and munched upon while it looked at Lee through the windshield. It had small black eyes, and Lee looked beyond it to an old man in a baggy brown cardigan watering his lawn. Lee'd been told that the wagtails were harbingers of a death in the family, and so he made sure to never look at one directly. His father was missing, presumed dead, but until a body was found, or a wagtail caught his eye, he wasn't going to accept the truth of what was obvious to everyone else.

The chitty-chitty danced and nodded its head and flew away so fast that when Lee blinked it was gone. Lee glanced in his side-mirror and drew his forearm off the window-rail just as a tyre iron smashed on the steel. Lee shrank back, turned and raised both legs and slammed them into the face of the man going for the passenger door. Lee swung and aimed for the driver's door, but it was open, and two arms grasped his legs and began to drag him out of the cab. He kicked hard, but there were hands on his throat from the passenger side and he was yanked from the cab, hitting his head on the way down. The kerb caught his back and knocked the wind out of him. He tried to roll over so that he could crawl under the truck, but the grip on his legs was strong. He saw the boot just before it struck his face. He got his hands up to ward off the next kick but that just meant his hand was smashed onto his nose, and then blood burst from his face and began to run into his eyes. He got both hands on the ground, and managed to grasp the front wheel and put his shoulder against it, taking another boot against his neck before launching his feet backwards and letting go of the tyre. His momentum took him over onto the toppled man, and he grabbed two fistfuls of cock and balls and squeezed until he heard the wail, then rolled off and ducked the next kick aimed at his head. The world slowed down now, as he knew that it would, as it always did. He dived and sank an elbow into the side of the prostrate man's head, and then he rolled into an awkward crouch, and when the other man came at him again he launched off to the side and caught him with a stiff-arm to the throat. Now they were all on the ground, and there was the tyre iron, and they were all getting up, and he leapt for the Ford and reached under the seat and pulled out the Luger. He didn't have time to turn the safety off but pointed it at them. The only movement was the water burbling out of the old man's hose. Lee clipped the safety off, took a gulp of air then kicked the tyre iron away. It was the same two men from the tow truck who'd given him fish-eyes near the freeway. The larger one in the shirtsleeves now spattered with Lee's blood was retching with ball-ache, while the other gasped for breath from his bruised windpipe. The buzzing in Lee's head was building. He felt himself start to fade into the red and he took another gulp of air to calm himself. The man across the road had dropped the hose and run inside; now it was snaking about and spraying the front-door screen.

Their tow truck was nowhere to be seen.

'Give me your wallets.'

They looked at him like he was stupid. He felt a surge of adrenalin and he was floating again and they saw the gun rise and reached for their back pockets at the same time.

'Drop 'em on the ground.'

He waved the Luger down the street. 'Now fuck off.'

They didn't need to be told. Lee turned his back on the sound of their footsteps, then scooped up the wallets. He did a lap of the truck, lifting up the number plates on their hinges. He snapped back the safety on the pistol and tossed in the wallets, got behind the wheel of the Ford. Out the corner of his eye he saw the chitty-chitty bird on the verge across the street and he nodded his head without looking at it and put the truck into gear.

4.

Lee assessed the damage as he drove down Canning Highway. Peeling off his t-shirt, he wiped his eyes clear of blood, making a smeary death mask of his face. He reached for his water bottle and tipped it over his head. His eyes stung but at least the next swipe with the t-shirt removed the pooled red around his eyes, even as it made clear the damage to his nose. He wiped the thicker blood from his nostrils but it continued to ooze. His heart was beating fast, and he tried to breathe slowly to allow his body's natural painkillers to replace the chemicals of fight and flight. There was a blackening gash on the bridge of his nose, which was askew. He held the t-shirt against his nose and applied pressure and looked into his eyes and saw that his pupils were dilated with shock. He began to concentrate again on his breathing, focussing on the details he'd scanned during the attack – the Celtic cross tattoo on the forearm of the bigger man, the small gold ring in his right ear and his bright blue eyes. The same crew cut as the thinner man, who had the same tattoo on his neck, tattoos on his knuckles that Lee hadn't been able to read. They both wore the same white cotton shirt with red and blue lines on its collar. The same brown workboots.

Lee removed the t-shirt from his face and the blood had stopped flowing from his nose. He wiped his face clean, snorted up the blood and hawked it out the window.

He was going to have to reset his nose. It was going to hurt. He looked instead at the bushfires burning in the hills, the muzzy brown haze to the north spreading from a roiling cloud of smoke that rose into the sky as far as he could see. The sun to his left was a glowing red orb. He began to pass fleabag motels and guessed that he was near the airport. He chose one at random and indicated across the lane of incoming traffic. He pulled into the cracked bitumen carpark and killed the engine, tipped the rest of the water over his face and watched it drain onto his shoulders.

*

The motel room was a painted breezeblock chamber with no windows, which stank of feet. The bed was made but there were curly black hairs on the pillow. Lee retrieved his swag from the truck, together with the Luger, a change of clothes and his first-aid kit. The desk jockey hadn't made any comment about Lee's rapidly swelling face and bare torso, just took the twenty dollars and handed over the key. Lee knew the story – the guy's pupils were dilated and his hair was gauzy on his dehydrated skull. Even as he talked, his jaw was set with an amphetamine lock. Lee had interrupted him cleaning the office with a vacuum cleaner, even though the carpet was spotless.

The mirror over the bathroom sink was the only clean surface in the room. Lee's eyes were already retreating behind the swelling that would soon blacken. He unspooled a wad of toilet paper and laid out the bandages and threaded the cotton through the stitching hook. The septum bone on the top of his nose where it became cartilage was skewed to the right. There was no easy way to do it. He ran the tap and took out the sink plug, then stood there for a while summoning the will to take his nose in a pinch-grip and before he knew it he was grabbing his nose between finger and thumb and crunching it into place. His nose began to bleed darkened clots, and then the blood was bright red. It dripped into the sink and he drew up running water and washed the blood off his face. The bones were back in alignment and he splashed his face and the mirror and the tiled wall that ran pink into the drain at his feet. He leaned over the sink and let the blood flow from his nose onto his mouth and chin. He took up the needle and thread, and beyond pain now, dug the hook through the torn flesh on the bridge of his nose. He pulled it taut until the knot bit and then he hooked it three more times, pulled the seam and tied it off. He hadn't breathed through the minute it took to apply the stitches, and now he cut off the remaining thread, wiped away the tears in his eyes and splashed his face clean. He poured iodine onto the cut and winced and swore at the sting. He pushed the wad of toilet paper up into his nostrils, tilted back his head and walked out of the bathroom. He fell down onto the swag, his head inclined over the back of his pillow as the blood drained into his throat. He smoked a cigarette with a shaky hand, and when his nerves were steady he reached into his duffel and drew out the letter.

Lee was careful not to get any blood on the letter. He scissored two fingers into the pink envelope with balloons floating on a streamer in one corner and a five-cent stamp in the other, postmarked Bicton. He drew out the letter that was written across three sheets of the same pink paper, with the same blue balloons in one corner. Lee knew the words by heart but he looked at the pages anyway, just to see Emma's writing. He would recognise those big rounded letters anywhere, especially the way she twirled the y's and g's. She wrote in a pale blue pen that matched the colour of the balloons, and despite the fact that the pages were unlined, her words didn't drift or run over the edges but continued in long sentences that awoke the sound of her voice in his head. She was writing to tell him that they'd found a rental place on the south side of the river, and that she was going to a Catholic girls school. Her uniform was a dark blue blazer with a light blue crest and dark stockings and skirt. She had to wear the uniform on the way to school and on the way back. The other girls were ok although they were pretty spoilt. None of them smoked pot and when they drank they danced for a while then keeled over. She missed hanging out with Lee at the drive-in. She missed his face. But she didn't miss Geraldton and would never go back.

Emma didn't need to mention why, and he could tell that she was forcing herself to be cheerful behind the pen that had dug into the paper. She said that she wished he'd write. She signed her name and added three x's. It was the signature and the three kisses that he returned to, time and again. You could see smudge marks where his fingers framed the page, on account of the hundreds of times he'd stared at those words and those kisses.

But he'd never written back.

Long ago he'd decided to go one better, and visit her instead.

Lee wasn't fit to visit anyone now, at least for a couple of weeks until his face improved. Emma's father had never liked him, and the sight of his mangled face would confirm his reasons for not wanting the two of them within a hundred miles of each other.

One of the first things that Emma's father had asked Lee was how his parents met. It was an odd question, and Lee hadn't been able to answer, because his father had always claimed that Lee's mother moved in with him the day he knocked her father down with a left hook in the red dirt yard of her Mullewa home. The man was a wife-beater who ogled his own daughter. The older man had gone and gotten his rifle, which he aimed at Lee's father's head while his daughter packed her bags. It didn't worry Lee's father – he ignored the man whose head was bleeding into his blue collared shirt. They drove into the setting sun in Lee's father's FJ Holden ute, and according to him, Mandy King had kissed his ear because finally she was free.

The plan was for Lee's face to heal, then to save money for a surfboard. Whether Emma's father liked it or not, he intended to invite her down to the Margaret River surf breaks that he'd only seen in mags – sculpted cold-water waves with barrels big enough that you could dance in. There was probably a school holiday coming soon. He didn't want to interrupt Emma's year twelve studies. She was going to be something – there wasn't any doubt about that.

Lee folded the sheets carefully because the paper-folds were starting to wear. He put the pages into the envelope and tried to drop the letter back into his duffel bag but missed, and it fell onto the carpet beside his head.

Never mind. His face was aching and his eyes were blurry. Some ice for his nose would be handy but he didn't want to get up. Tomorrow he'd ice his face and clean up the stitches properly. He was lucky that his nose had copped the blow and not his teeth.

Lee closed his eyes and let himself drift backwards into the throbbing of his face. There was no darkness there but only a red cloud that filled his ears with static. He let himself go until the pain was diffuse enough to not feel it. He felt his limbs go heavy, and he focused on his breathing. He watched the light change on his eyelids as night came, and he sniffed and realised that his face had hardened into a mask. He was thinking about his father's story from when he was locked in Fremantle Prison, and how the screws came to give him a beating after lockdown, every night for a month. He'd made them earn their licks, he said, and as soon as he heard the door-lock turn he'd get up on his bed in the corner so that he could kick and narrow the range of their baton-attack. It was a strange memory, until Lee heard the lock turn in the motel room door and then his blood was pumping and his eyes were open and he was rolling, but there was no back door to escape from. He got up on the bed and backed into the corner as the hands reached out to grab him. His eyes were still blurry, and he kicked out at the arms that were trying to get at his legs to drag him off the bed. He connected with a snap-kick and heard the *oompf* as the man went out, and then he was swinging the bedside lamp with the cord still attached and the bulb shattered over the shoulder of another man who'd strode across the back of his unconscious friend like he was a footpath. Lee didn't recognise any of the men in the darkened room and there were two more coming at him and there was an older man leaning in the doorframe smoking a cigarette and watching with a smile. Lee's nose began to bleed again, and his chin was slick with blood and then he felt a pain in his side and his legs turned to jelly. He looked down at the weapon that had paralysed him in the hand of the grinning man and it looked like a torch. All movement had stopped in the room and the man leaned in and stuck Lee in the side again and the electric shock was like a belt around the head with a steel chair.

Two sets of arms ripped him to the floor. There was a boot on the back of his head and another on his ankles. The electric shock was gone but his heart was still lurching.

'Watch it, Ballard, he's got more tricks. Can see it in his eyes.'

It was the older man, who closed the door behind him.

'Tie him up. This is no ordinary kid. You got army training, young fella?'

The blood from Lee's nose was soaking into the carpet while cable ties closed around his hands as the older man navigated the crush of bodies and came into view, peering into the bathroom before turning and looking at Lee. 'My name is Kinslow. I run a towing service with a fleet of ten tow trucks and flatbeds. I see you sewed yourself up pretty good. I'll ask again. You got military training?'

Lee didn't reply, just stared at the older man. He wore black jeans and workboots, a black button-down shirt and a navy jacket. Black peaked cap. Grey hair and a goatee beard. A heavy gold watch on his wrist.

'Toss his things. Empty that duffel bag and give me his wallet.'

Lee had hidden the Luger beneath the mattress but they already knew he was armed. His duffel was tipped onto the floor in a jumble of jeans and t-shirts and a box of ammunition and, last of all, his books; five, six, then more, hard and softbacks until all dozen books were piled and splayed open.

The old man whistled, got down on his haunches and picked up a paperback, showed Lee the cover. 'You like this book, son?'

It was *The Turner Diaries*, his father's thumbed copy. Lee ignored the older man and thought instead about Emma's letter, and how he might kick it under the bed. The man stayed crouched, and took Lee's wallet, extracted his driver's licence. There was a curious light in his eyes as he looked at the licence and compared it to Lee's face.

'Boys, I've got to make a call. Hold the young fella but try not to hurt him any more than necessary. Use the cattle prod if required but leave his face alone. He already looks like hamburger.'

*

The older man, Kinslow, was gone for a long time. Lee stood with his hands bound, trying to be brave. The blood was drying in his nose but he couldn't wipe it away or settle the itch. He figured he was due some more beating. The reality was that he'd been naïve to think that he could rock up in the city and operate his rig, without stepping on toes. The young men were eager to lay into him, he could tell. The nearest stood before him with the cattle prod inches from Lee's belly, and his breath stank of stale coffee and his eyes were yellow in the semi-dark. He was broad across the shoulders and although he'd beefed up his arms he was also quick on his feet. Like the man who had Lee by the scruff, he was probably a tow driver too. Lee could feel the workingman calluses scraping the back of his neck, the hand loose in case the prod was used again. There was another man going through his duffel bag. He was taking his time about it, tossing Lee's clothes onto the bed so irregularly that he realised they were looking for something specific. They were all dressed in the same polo shirts, branded with a red laurel wreath on its breast. The young man with the yellow eyes wore blue jeans and workboots, but when he saw that Lee was watching him he tucked in his shirt that had been loosened in the struggle,

44

ran a hand over his shaved head and stared with dead eyes.

'You got me good,' Lee said. 'Made your point. Give me my keys and I'll be on my way. I was always gonna head over east.'

'Good try, mate. But don't think so.'

It was the first time any of them had spoken, apart from the older man. The accent was broad Australian.

'Why not?' Lee said. 'I made a mistake. I'll go find somewhere else to work.'

The young man laughed. 'This ain't about towin, and turf. Not anymore. Not since Kinslow got here. This is about APM matters now.'

'I don't know what that is,' said Lee. 'Got nothing to do with me.'

Yellow eyes seemed to take offence at that, peeled up the sleeve of his polo. A tattooed swastika, and beneath that the letters APM, in Gothic font. 'APM. Australian Patriotic Movement. You with me now?'

Lee hadn't heard of the APM beyond his father's stories about what was happening in Perth: vague anecdotes about badly organised right-wingers who thought that plastering posters across the city was the way forward. Skinheads and hoons going the bash against blacks and Asians. A few crazed plotters and rumours of blowing up this and that.

'What's that yer standin on?'

'Just a letter.'

'Move off it.'

Lee didn't move and so the man before him smiled and pushed the sliding button on the cattle prod whose twin elements began to crackle. He stuck the thing in Lee's belly and, although his guts were tensed, the shock was like a punch to his heart and he felt it in his teeth and against the back of his skull.

But it didn't move him, and he felt the grip on the back of his neck tighten. 'Do 'im agin.'

Yellow eyes winked over Lee's shoulder, and he felt the grip leave his neck as the man put the prod against his crotch and stood back and watched. The pain was worse than any kick to the balls, and his knees buckled and his guts came up inside him. He swallowed on the gorge in his throat which tasted of acid and coffee. Then the hand was back on his neck and they threw him facedown onto the bed. It was just a moment before he got his face raised off his clothes, but Lee felt it, and understood that there were worse things than a beating to come. His jeans were still belted up but the atmosphere in the room had changed. He remembered the letter, and turned to watch the grinning fool who was kneeling down reading in the small halo from the bathroom light. There was a knee in Lee's back now, and the prod was at his throat. He was forced to kneel and watch the stupid smile and hear Emma's words in the mouth of the idiot.

They kept him kneeling for thirty minutes, his eyes on the bedside alarm clock. Every time Lee asked a question the men ignored him.

Finally, he heard the key turn in the door.

'Get off him.'

Lee's wrists were levered and then he was on his feet.

'Bring that chair and tie him.'

There was a flurry of movement as hands reached to their task. The other man, Kinslow, had returned. He tossed a roll of gaffer tape to the one who'd been reading Emma's letter, then reached into his pocket and drew out a black cotton bag. He flapped it open and leaned over and forced it onto Lee's head.

Then everything went quiet in the room. All Lee could hear was breathing. The door to the room opened. He sensed something near his face, and then someone walking around him. The voice, when it came, was warm in his right ear. It was the voice of a very old man. English accent, with a touch of something else.

'We know who you are, Lee. And who your father is. Towing is a small community and I'm surprised he'd encourage you to do it, knowing our interests here. So I'll assume that you've done this yourself. We can't let you work our streets and freeways, but if you answer my questions, honestly and respectfully, we might just let you leave in one piece. Do you understand?'

Lee nodded because there was nothing else to do. There were questions of his own that needed answering, but they could wait.

The old man hadn't left his position by Lee's right ear. 'We know that your father is missing, presumed ... six feet under. I knew your father. I won't do you the dishonour of asking about him, or Knights operational matters. I only want to know one thing. One important thing that I hope you'll appreciate is good for the cause. We want to know where your father sourced his weapons. I've seen his armoury, and we've done some trade in the past. I know what he's buried out in the desert. I don't want any of that. I don't want trouble with what's left of the Knights. I want a name. A contact. So that I can build on what your father started.'

There was something about the man's voice that was frightening. The precise laying out of words, reflecting the clarity of his thinking and seeing. Lee knew that the man was serious, even if the others were clowns.

'Fuck off,' Lee said quietly, trying to muster the same calm determination, the same projection of authority.

'Good boy. *Good* boy. Fair play to you.'

Lee listened to the rustling of silk as the man stood, and moved away. He heard the sound of a zippo lighter and the creak of boot-leather as another man knelt beside him. It started as a warmth on the back of his thigh, behind the knee, then he smelled burning denim and then the pain was hot and his jeans were on fire and his skin was screaming. There were no hands on his shoulders and he felt himself float to his feet and his vision faded to a speckled red and then he was swinging the chair like a steel tail and butting with his head and his eyes were saturated with the red and then he was gone.

5.

Lee Southern was awake and there was light on his eyelids. Before he moved or opened his eyes he floated in the warmth and stillness that would soon be disturbed by pain. He didn't know if he'd been unconscious for one minute or a day. He listened, and all he could hear was wattlebirds squawking outside a window and the wind pushing branches over a tin roof. The air was cool on his body and he understood that he was naked. There was no pain, even when he clenched his fingers, and turned his neck. No throb or ache or shrill signal from his skin, even though he knew that he'd been burned.

He opened his eyes.

The bedroom was empty.

The door to the large room with unpainted jarrah skirts and architraves was open. His books were on a shelf above an empty fireplace. His clothes were folded inside an ancient-looking wardrobe, alongside his boots. His duffel bag was on top of the wardrobe.

Lee rolled onto his feet. The linen on the bed was fresh

and there were spare pillows on the jarrah floorboards. Now the headache came on behind his eyes. It wasn't the usual concussion headache but something else. There was a nasty chemical smell in his sinuses and he remembered the smell of ether from his father's field kit. On the bedside table were a digital alarm clock and a pill bottle. He looked closer and the label said morphine sulphate and the bottle was empty. There was powder on the varnished wood and he looked at his arms and saw that he'd been injected. There was no trace of the needle.

He was bruised all over, but couldn't feel it. On one of his thighs was a handprint bruise that looked like an ochre painting on a cave wall, and he reached under his leg where he'd been burned and found a bandage squishy with salve.

He put his fingers on his nose and understood that the stitches had been replaced with butterfly strips.

The wattlebirds outside his window had ceased their bickering and he could hear traffic. He drew back the white curtains and copped the sun in his face. He put up an arm and waited until his eyes stopped watering. The way his headache was developing, it was a pity the pill bottle was empty. He padded over to the cupboards and slipped into some red jocks. They were from a packet of ten that his father had bought last year to share with him. They all went into the same wash so it didn't make much difference.

Lee put on his spare jeans. He'd lost weight and needed a belt and he looked around for the jeans they'd set on fire. The jeans were gone but the belt was hung over the back of a chair. He threaded the links and tightened it an extra notch. He found Emma's letter in his duffel. One of the folds had torn, but every page was there.

There were two other bedrooms but only one was used; the ceiling fan turning quietly and sheets draped onto the floorboards. There was nobody in the bathroom or kitchen and he went out the back door, shielding his eyes from the sun. It was a regular parched yard with asbestos fencing, a Hills hoist and lemon tree, and an asbestos shed in the corner. There was an outside dunny against the back fence which told Lee that they were in an older suburb. The lawn was a tangle of couch grass and the dirt beneath it was grey. The houses on either side had tall bloodwood eucalypts in their yards.

There was a noise behind him.

It was the girl from the tow truck – hard to forget that dark asymmetrical hair and pale skin. She stood on the back steps in knickers and a baggy t-shirt, sipping a glass of orange juice. She had tattoos on her thighs of jaguar heads but it was her eyes that caught his attention. Despite the fierce sunlight, they were big and grey. Empty of every expression except curiosity.

'They said I have to stay here and comfort you.'

Her accent was posh, like the voices on the government radio.

'Thanks.'

She finished her drink and nodded. 'The amount of smack in your blood, you'll be comfortable for days.'

Some mirth in her eyes, watching for his reaction.

'Did you fix me up?'

'I'm a nurse.'

'Did I talk?'

'Sorry?'

He stared at her, but she never left his eyes. She hadn't been there at the hotel room, when he'd gone berserk.

'Why are you looking after me? Why were you told to *comfort* me?'

'You'll have to ask Kinslow that. There's a note for you on the microwave. I'm going to shower and get ready for work. I've extracted some codeine that's filtering on the benchtop in there. You can drink it anytime, but only half.'

'This your place?'

She didn't answer him, beyond tipping the dregs of her drink in the dirt, turning back inside. He watched her walk down the hall.

The note was written on a postcard of Perth, taken from Kings Park. It was propped on his truck keys, which he scooped and pocketed. Written in a clear hand, the card read: *Stay here as long as you wish. This is a safe house and it's yours. I've added the front door key to your keyring. If you run, we'll find you.*

Lee went to the room and tossed his things. Everything there except what he was looking for – his Luger.

The woman was dressed now in jeans and a baggy green jumper. Riding boots. Running a brush through her hair, framed by an edge of light around the heavy drapes.

'Like I said, Kinslow will be back tonight.'

'You didn't tell me your name.'

'You didn't ask, or tell me yours.'

'My name's Lee … Southern.'

She laughed. 'I know what it is. My name's Frankie.'

'Frankie.'

'For Francesca.'

Which explained the dark hair and eyes.

'Can I help you, Lee?'

He realised he'd been staring. Frankie brushing her hair was a simple domestic moment, but then again he'd grown up in a house without women.

'They've got something of mine. I want to be on my way, but …'

Now she looked concerned. 'You can't leave.'

'Because you're supposed to keep me here. Comforted.'

She tossed her brush onto the unmade bed. Stood square on, then softened her posture, stroked her hair and wrapped a strand around her fingers, put on a girlish voice. 'Is that what you want? To be comforted?'

She was good.

'I don't want anything from you. I don't have anything you want, either. I just …'

She crossed the room and took his arm, led him into the corridor. He let himself be led, could hardly feel his feet on the boards or the touch of her fingers. She guided him into a bathroom and stood him in front of the mirror.

His face.

A livid pulpy mess.

Unrecognisable, except for his eyes, slitted through the

black swelling.

'So there you are. They nearly had to kill you, I was told. I don't know what they want from you, and I don't care. But you need to rest up.'

'How long was I –'

'Two days.'

He looked at her reflection in the mirror. She didn't look away.

'I put your books on the shelf. The usual shit, but also Blake. Keats. Nietzsche too. *Thus Spake Zarathustra*. I'm intrigued. Have you read them all?'

Lee nodded, but it was a lie.

'Come with me. I'll bring morphine tonight, but in the meantime, codeine will have to do.'

In the kitchen Frankie lifted off a sopping filter from over a glass, wadded it and tossed it in the bin. 'That much paracetamol would blow your liver. But here, drink this.'

The liquid was bitter and he lifted the glass until he felt her hand on his arm.

'Easy, tiger, I said half. There's twenty Panadeine Forte's worth of codeine in that glass. We don't want you OD'ing.'

Lee put the glass on the bench. Frankie passed him a mug of water to cleanse the bitterness.

He allowed himself to be led into the yard. He stood there like a docile child while she carried over a chair for him to sit in. He planted himself and sprawled, tilted his face into the sun.

'Anybody else, I'd park them in the shade. But you, you're so tanned. I envy you.'

Her voice came from a long way away, or somewhere underwater, or from behind the cumulus clouds that scudded to the horizon.

'You said they nearly killed me. Why didn't they?' he asked, unsure whether the sounds had made it out his mouth.

'And I said I didn't know. I guess they want something from you.'

She was close, seated in the shade beside him, and he opened his eyes.

'What do they want from *you*?' he asked. 'Why are you here? Are you with the ... APM?'

She didn't answer him. She was looking at something in her lap that interested her more. 'I'm interested in this book. Instead of *Mein Kampf*, you have this.'

Lee's eyes had closed, and it was too much to open them. 'They're my father's books. We, him ... we're not fascists. We're not even nationalists. We just don't trust the state. Nazi Germany was just another oligarchic state that guaranteed the enrichment of a few billionaires.'

'That's an impressive vocab. You didn't learn those opinions at school.'

The change of tack confused him. 'My mother was into books. She taught me to read early, before I went to school.'

'What about this one? Have you read it? It's *Michael Bakunin: Selected Writings*.'

Fortunately, a book that Lee had read to his father often. He heard himself begin to speak. 'You and I, we weren't made for living like this.' Eyes closed, Lee lifted a hand and wafted it at the suburbs. The best he could do. 'Ever since the industrial revolution, anarchism is the best response we have to state socialism, and to corporate capitalism. We aim to live in communes of like-minded people. Freedom for ourselves and respect for others like us. Recognising the power of no state or government but our own community.'

Lee had been speaking automatically, and by the time he finished he'd forgotten where he started, or the reason why he'd been speaking. It was all rote learning from his father's lessons. He struggled to open his eyes, but couldn't. His limbs felt moulded to the chair. He was numb and euphoric at once, only the cool air in his lungs a sign that he was alive.

'Just, wow.'

Whatever he'd said, it made an impression.

'We didn't have a television at home,' he said. 'Just books.'

'You're so naïve … *brainwashed*.'

Now Lee opened his eyes. Frankie smiling, but no friendliness there, her eyes cool with malice, and something even more hurtful – disappointment.

'Kinslow's guys,' she said. 'They're kind of comical. Like boys playing soldiers. But you, you really believe that stuff. You must've had some upbringing. I feel sorry for you.'

Lee struggled. Did he believe what he'd said?

Frankie didn't look at him as she stood to leave.

*

It was dark when he awoke. Someone had draped a blanket over his shoulders and his feet were hot. He hadn't noticed the fire-pit earlier in the day, but now it was heaped with glowing coals. Lengths of jarrah sleeper were laid across it giving off orange licks and what was that smell?

Beside the fire-pit was a smouldering fence post. It was blackened and paint-blistered and someone had put it on the fire. Someone had also taken it out.

In the light of the fire he saw the dried bauble of blood on his forearm and realised that he'd been injected again. He didn't mind, instead rolled his neck, felt a rush of nausea and staggered toward the nearest tree and vomited a thin gruel.

A hand on his shoulder. Not leaving as he retched. Patting him like a mother.

'Frankie?'

'No lad, she's at work wiping arses and nicking pills. Our own twisted Florence Nightingale.'

When there was nothing left in Lee's stomach, the hand lifted from his shoulder. He turned and looked into the face of the man called Kinslow. Salt-and-pepper goatee beard, eyes flickering with reflected light.

'Now do you want me to tuck you into bed, or would you prefer to come and join our brotherhood?'

There was nothing in Kinslow's eyes to confirm the implicit mockery, only the same look that Lee recognised from just about every man he'd known – predatorily reading him for weakness.

'Some of the boys wanted to mess with you, out here alone by the fire, after what you did to them earlier. Can you manage to walk?'

Yes, he could walk, and more. 'Give me my Luger, and I'll be on my way.'

A dark flare went off in Kinslow's eyes, but only for a moment, and the smile never left his face.

'Can I call you Lee?'

'I'm serious about the Luger. You're gonna want to –'

'Shut the fuck up, *boy*. We plan on giving it to you, on the condition that you tell the lads the story behind it. Some of them have got SS daggers and German helmets and the like, but your gun is something else. Indulge 'em, and I'll give it back.'

'I can do that.'

'Good. They told me you're clever.'

Lee drew the blanket around his shoulders and scuffed sand off his feet, following Kinslow through the back door into the brightly lit house that was loud with laughter and music.

There were a few young men in the kitchen who watched him closely. They wore stovepipe jeans and tight-fitting Bonds t-shirts. They didn't look particularly hard, sipping on cans of Emu and smoking. He could tell from their body language that they were close friends, and the fact that they were away from the noise coming from the front room told Lee where they fitted in.

The floorboards in the corridor trembled.

'The English,' Kinslow muttered, 'they got to dance and sing.'

It was music like Lee had never heard before, fast and heavy, overlaid with enough singing voices that he couldn't tell the singer from those singing along. The chorus was about stealing and then he was in the room and Kinslow nudged the wall-socket by the door, killing the tape deck.

There were a dozen or so arm in arm in the middle of the room, and a couple didn't realise that the music had ended.

Their voices tapered off and they turned to Kinslow, then looked Lee up and down. Some of them wore baggy woollen pants and braces, others jeans and those collared white shirts. Two were shirtless and the Celtic cross tattoo was on their arms and chest. Some were pasty and overweight and others were dark and lean. Some had short hair and some had long. The three who'd bashed him were seated on an overstuffed chintz couch in the corner. One sported a black eye, another had his fist bandaged. The biggest one, who'd applied the cattle prod, hid his smirk, and like the other two got to his feet, clearly acting under orders and reluctant about it. They pushed through the dancers and came to Lee, thrusting out their hands to shake.

'Terry, Gaz, Robbie … this is Lee Southern. I know you've met but this time you meet as comrades. Equals. Stronger in unity and all that.'

There was a knock on the front door and Kinslow left and the music started up again. Like a game of statues, those in the room resumed their dancing. Lee shook hands with the three young men. The biggest one leaned in.

'I'm Robbie. It's our job to show you round, take you out on the road with us. It's *my* job to get rid of you, if you fuck up.'

He squeezed the bones in Lee's hand. His breath smelled of chip oil. His eyes were bloodshot.

Lee smiled. You never telegraph a crime, even to friends, even as a warning, unless you're an idiot.

Lee took his hand back and let his eyes drift across the crowd of dancing and drinking men. Robbie reminded him of Danny Hislop, an old enemy. The same dull eyes and fighter's swagger, leaning forward as though eager to attack. Danny Hislop was in Lee's class at school and they'd grown up together in the Knights' family. Despite this, they'd always been rivals. 'Keep away from that prick,' his father always said. 'He's got that look in his eye. In the old days they'd take a boy like that into the woods and put an arrow into him, or club him to death. Hunting accident, or a falling branch. Push him off the edge of an ice floe, walk him into a peat bog, or slit his throat and put it down to a snapped fence wire. So that his mother didn't feel like she'd borne a monster.'

Jack Southern had been right about Danny, that was for sure. The reason Lee was now in Perth. The reason Emma had moved back to the city.

Because Lee was ignoring him, Robbie put an arm around his shoulder, gave him a little bump. Most men take a lot of working up to reach a state where they can hurt someone, but that look in Robbie's eye – he was always ready. The meaty arm sat heavy on Lee's shoulders, a moment or a whim away from a choke-lock, but Lee didn't shrug it off – he didn't have anything to prove.

The music died again. Kinslow had returned. 'Alright, Village People. Time for the poster-units to go to work. You know your sectors and your team leaders have the muster points should you get separated. All weapons get left here, and that is an order. Especially you Pommy blokes – knives get left here. We don't want any negative publicity now that the election's coming. Should it come to that – ambush by Bogs or Abos – then you'll need to be resourceful and fall back on your training. In an urban environment there's weapons everywhere if you know where to look. Team leaders meet back at the depot at o-five hundred hours. Let's get the message out there. Go!'

The room cleared and then it was just the five of them: the three youths, Lee and Kinslow. Robbie and his two mates looked like the cats who got the cream. They hadn't been sent out to glue up posters through the night. Robbie still had an arm around Lee's shoulder, and Lee shrugged it off to face Kinslow, who was cupping his hand around a cigarette, prison style.

Kinslow nodded, smiled. Reached behind his belt and drew out Lee's pistol, passed the Luger over butt-first. Lee took it and popped out the magazine and saw that it was empty. Nothing in the chamber either.

'I put 'em in the drawer by your bed.'

Handing back Lee's gun was a surprise to the other three. They looked at it enviously. Lee clapped the magazine in and passed it to Terry, the smallest one, whose green eyes and red hair and creamy skin made him resemble a painted statue. He stuck his tongue out the side of his mouth and pointed the gun at Gaz, the second one, who laughed, because everyone saw him flinch.

'No offence to Lee, but that's why I removed the bullets. Stupid there can't be trusted.'

Kinslow's insult stung, and Terry handed the Luger to Gaz, shifting their attention off him. Robbie pretended to be uninterested, but had taken on an oddly formal posture, like a soldier stood down but waiting for orders.

'Wonder how many Jews this little baby's shot?' Gaz asked.

Kinslow looked to Lee, who nodded. 'My grandfather took it off a German officer outside Tobruk.'

'SS?'

'German Africa Corps.'

'They was brave men,' Robbie said, 'Rommel's soldiers at the Siege of Tobruk. Some of 'em got their livers eaten by Maori, I heard. What happened to the officer?'

'Lee's grandfather shot him. With that pistol. Right in the head. Isn't that right, Lee?'

Lee looked into Kinslow's eyes, who'd obviously heard the story before. Again he wondered – the delirious past days and nights – how much he had said.

'I knew … know your father. We were in Vietnam together. At Balmoral.'

Lee looked to Kinslow with a renewed interest, because Lee's father wasn't the only Knight to serve with the 3 RAR. 'You in contact with other Knights?'

'I am. Yes.'

There was enough in Kinslow's eyes to make Lee take the Luger off Robbie, who was weighing it in his hand, sighting into the fireplace. Out of habit, Lee held the Luger by his side, semi-concealed. He'd wondered why they were looking after him – now he knew.

'Don't worry, son. I know what you did, and I know they're looking for you. I told Greg Downs that I hadn't seen you, but that I'd keep an eye out.'

Greg Downs, who'd stepped in to take Jack Southern's position as president of the Knights. Who most people believed had killed Lee's father, to avenge the death of his brother Brady Downs, found buried in the dunes behind Lee's family block on the Greenough River. The police were led there by Brady's burnt-out Statesman, found in some bushes not far away.

'He know my wheels?'

'He figures you're driving a Sandman. That you've probably gone bush, but just in case, got the word out.'

Kinslow was telling the truth but he had plenty of reasons to lie. Greg Downs would love to get his hands on Lee, while Kinslow would get a good deal to hand him over. Some of those weapons the Knights had famously hidden in the bush.

Lee didn't like the look in Robbie's eyes. 'What?'

Robbie looked to Kinslow. 'He comin with us?'

Kinslow shook his head. 'He isn't right, yet ...'

This appeared to please the other two, but it made Robbie even more suspicious.

Kinslow saw this and grunted. 'Nor is he ready. You're going to rest up here, aren't you, Lee?'

Lee had no intention of resting up. Now that he had the Luger, he could get back on the road. Start again where nobody knew him.

'The boys and I have some things to discuss. A bit of privacy, thanks Lee. How 'bout you go to your room for a bit.'

That made Robbie swell with pride. He sneered at Lee's shrug and retreat out the door, even as the others gathered around Kinslow, who dropped his voice and leaned in.

*

Lee got himself a glass of tap water and lit a cigarette and went back to his room. He smoked the cigarette in hard tugs. He prodded his nose in front of the mirror and felt nothing. It was going to hurt like hell when the drugs wore off. He could see from the thick line of bruising beneath his right eye socket that his cheekbone was fractured too.

On the dresser by his bed was a single morphine pill. So Kinslow knew that he was leaving, didn't want to supply him enough to set him free.

Lee necked the pill. He went to the shelves and swiped his books into his duffel bag. Did the same to his stacked clothes in the cupboard. Knelt to his boots and felt around for Emma's letter, which was there.

Kinslow and his boofheads were gone. The front door was open to a weedy lawn flattened by tyre marks. Lee's Ford was parked on the verge. He went to it and found the door unlocked. He keyed the ignition, and the engine turned over but wouldn't spark. Kinslow had immobilised it – taken out the rotor arm or ignition leads. Lee went inside the house and began to search, starting with Francesca's room. There were boxes in her cupboard that he took down but the smell of mothballs made him nauseous. The pill was kicking in and his feet felt like they were snowshoes. A creamy warmth spread through his limbs and his head was dizzy. He made a half-hearted tour of the hallway, rapping his knuckles on the floorboards, looking for that cache-board he'd been told was always present in old homes. It was only when he returned to consciousness with his head against a doorframe and drool on his chin that he realised how high he'd gone. He stayed on his hands and knees and crawled to bed.

6.

Lee was awake but his body was asleep. Or his mind was separate from his body. Or his mind was floating unhampered by the noise of his body that wasn't sending signals of pain or sensation. He just wanted to lie there and close his eyes and float on the cushion of euphoria that made him not care about anything that'd happened over the past days, or the days that were coming. He hadn't learned anything new about the APM except that they were organised enough to field candidates in an election. They wanted something from him beyond the source of his father's weaponry contact, which he didn't know anyway, and so couldn't tell them.

Lee lifted his foot from the bed and the effort was too much and that was because he was part of the bed and suffered the extra gravity of the bed. He would have liked to try this drug out in the desert. He'd taken acid a few times with his father out in the desert after a period of meditation where they'd sat beside an old riverbed that was pocked with the prints of goat, emu and kangaroo. The most recent time, a year ago now, Lee had cradled his grandfather's .303 in his lap. His senses were alert to every sound and movement in the poverty bushes and the pink everlastings that carpeted the red dirt. Above them, the pale salmon gums were tall and still and watching them right back. The meditation was something that his father had learned in Vietnam from a buddy who was military intelligence, and who went on raiding parties with the SAS and 3 RAR companies when they were out in the bush for two weeks at a time. For every moment of those two weeks they maintained silence as they crept through the jungle or hid in the rocks and waited for their enemy. Two weeks of silence and just watching and listening. Two weeks of eating cold rations, and not smoking, and burying their waste like cats. Some men cracked under the weight of the silence and began to shake and mutter, or else they ground their teeth at night and had to be gently smothered back into wakefulness. Two weeks of silence and night terrors and then back to base for two days of drunken R&R and then back out into the jungle for two more weeks of hunting the enemy. Like that for the entire twelve-month tour; two weeks of hunting and two days of R&R. Two weeks of hunting and two days of R&R.

Lee's father passed him the microdot of acid after they'd sat there on the riverbank in silence for an hour. 'You wait and see, son. The fish desires eyes that see at night and the fish develops eyes that see at night. When we focus our will on this place right here, then it'll respond to us.'

An hour later, Lee watched the kangaroo enter the riverbank down a hollow eaten by the last floods. The dry riverbed opened into a braid of channels where snagged branches created a hide that the doe hopped around before twitching its ears and looking at them. Lee had never seen a kangaroo behave this way. It hopped closer and the acid in Lee's blood began to surge and the dappled light around them began to blend with the wind. Lee's father was absolutely still. The kangaroo doe came to a stop five metres away, looking up at Lee with moist black eyes that said nothing. He looked to his father, who nodded. Lee closed his right eye and sighted with his left. He squeezed the trigger of the antique rifle and the muzzle blast reached out and struck the kangaroo down. It lay there, shot in the head, only one foot twitching to say that it had ever lived.

His father's knife left its sheath with a scrape. He walked down to the doe and hoisted it upon his shoulder. 'I'll dress her. You stay and think on what you've just witnessed, and what I told you.'

No sooner had his father gone than Lee began to doubt what had happened. He looked at his bare feet on the red dirt. He smelled the campfire and pulled his knees up to his chin. Then he was walking, and then he was inside his great-grandfather's shack, built in the 1890s out of jamwood boughs and flattened kerosene cans sewn together with wire. The corrugated iron roof was a single pitch against the northern sun. Dirt floor and scraps of hessian to cover the internal wall. A couple of rough-hewn stools and a sheared granite sheet that formed a table, perched on mulga boughs that had rusted tin cans at their base. Fill the cans with water and strands of tobacco to keep the ants off the table.

Lee sat on the stool and watched his father tend the fire, laying slices of roo meat into his smoking-frame.

The hearth that had warmed four generations of Southerns.

Away from the fire was a midden of sardine cans and ancient beer and medicine bottles, ceramic shards and rusted shovelheads. A pile of silvered sandalwood branches and sticks, dragged from the surrounding bush over decades and slowly added to the fire. Lee's grandfather, Vernon Southern, gone religious with the isolation, had taken to the blacks' habit of shrouding a young Jack Southern's head with sandalwood smoke for the purposes of warding away the devils that gathered around lonely folk. Lee's grandfather was a Tobruk rat and gold fossicker who sometimes bound himself hand and foot and smashed his bullets because he couldn't shake the desire to shoot himself.

Which was why Lee's father had grown up mostly with his uncle Cosmo in the wheatbelt town of Dalwallinu, so that he could get some schooling. The government people had heard about a boy living in the bush with his old father and come looking for him. When Lee's father returned to the camp one weekend afternoon, having walked the thirty K cross-country from Paynes Find, he found his father Vernon kneeling and praying before a hand-whittled Jesus of Nazareth perched on a trunk of rivergum. Beside him was a hammer, and the trunk was stained red. Vernon had nailed his hand to the wood. Lee's father had kicked Vernon Southern in the buttocks and with tears in his eyes demanded that he move into town and cease all the foolishness. Vernon could barely croak, and Lee's dad had knelt down beside his father and joined him in prayer.

'Son, God can see into my heart and he told me that I got to kill that part of me that wants to kill, and I don't know any other way. I'm not fit to live in town until I get this done. Till I quench those pictures in my head. Till I douse that voice. Say after me ... Lord, hear my prayer ...'

But Vernon Southern had returned to town, where his head cleared up with the help of cheap wine, regular work and a caring brother.

*

Now that the slices of kangaroo taken from the backstrap and leg were hot-smoking above the fire, Lee watched his father cut away the pale tendons from the heels and place them into a cup of water, for softening. He was making another longbow and needed the tendons and sinew for fixings. He cut out the rump from the pelvic frame and placed it into the camp oven, fixed the lid and laid it on the bed of coals he'd dragged from the fire, shovelled more coals on the lid. The rump would cook overnight, to be carved for breakfast and lunch tomorrow.

His father was singing some old rockabilly number in a deliberate country voice, making up words he didn't know. Lee lit a cigarette and wiped his eyes with the back of his hands and looked to the sunset and longed for the cooler night air. His blood and the desert air were at the same temperature, and in the windless clearing it made him feel like he was underwater.

He'd just turned sixteen, and this wasn't the first time he'd taken acid with his father, but on those other occasions his father talked him through it. There were no hallucinations this time, and he was grateful for that. He felt like being alone, walking up onto the nearest granite monolith from where he could see horizon to horizon in every direction across the mulga scrub and not a puff of smoke or sign of human presence. But the caves along the nearest rock face were spooky even during the daytime, and he couldn't imagine being alone there at night.

There were hearths in those caves that had been used for so many centuries that the coarse red granite had melted to form a smooth blackened bowl. Handprints of different sizes on the walls, using the red and yellow ochre from the mine at Wilgie Mia that the blacks had dug out over thirty millennia, using scaffolding to get down into their pits and tunnels. According to his father, it was the oldest mine in the world, the ochre traded around Australia, right through the five hundred or so tribes that peopled the continent. Lee wondered whether the men and women who made the hand-paintings in the cave felt proud of that fact, or ever got to see the blood of their earth on other walls in other lands. He knew that they were called Badimaya but no more than that. A more numerous people had come across the oceans and taken their land from them, and that was the reason the Knights had formed. That was the reason he and his father were out in the desert, among the spectral presences of the earlier people, which was a constant reminder of what would happen to them too if they weren't ready.

When Lee asked why Great-grandpa Donal Southern made his camp in the bush away from the rock, instead of using the cave system that was cool even in the heat of day, his father shook his head and replied that if Lee couldn't figure that out, then he should spend a night sleeping there. Lee knew that the blacks had been cleared out by rifle and poison, and that those who remained were carted away in the back of a truck. 'Was there blacks here when Vernon's father Donal came in the eighteen nineties?' he asked instead.

'Sure there were,' Lee's father had replied. 'How do you think he survived out here?'

'So it wasn't him that did the clearing out?'

'That was the cattlemen. They came later. With their empire laws.'

Donal, Vernon, Jack and Lee Southern. Four generations of Southerns who'd camped on this dirt, the first two generations living here while looking for gold. Donal the only one who had any luck, and that was because he'd been shown where to look. The story told to Lee was that, for reasons unknown, the blacks used to put nuggets at the base of trees. All Donal had to do was walk through the parklike woodland and pick 'em up, like a child's Easter-egg hunt.

Lee tried to imagine what it must've been like for Donal Southern, a convict from Glasgow who'd slaved in Perth quarrying limestone before getting his ticket. Who'd walked his wheelbarrow the four hundred miles from the coast to Kalgoorlie when the first strike was made. Who'd stayed in the desert for the rest of his life, wandering from field to field, until Vernon was born on this very spot. Lee's great-grandmother dying in childbirth, her grave under a cairn not twenty metres from where Lee sat.

'How did Great-grandpa Donal give milk to Grandpa Vernon, when he was a newborn?'

Lee's father had always encouraged knowledge of their ancestors. He felt it was important to understand what they'd been through. Lee'd asked the same question before, using different words, but never got a straight answer.

'I don't know, son. I really don't know.'

Lee tried to imagine Grandpa Vernon Southern growing up barefoot and wild out there with no mother and no schooling. Both of them, Donal and Vernon, squatting on some cattleman's station that they didn't know the extent of, because it didn't matter.

It was Vernon Southern who first left Donal's camp as a boy and moved to work the marginal wheat country around Northampton, and then the fishing boats off Geraldton. Didn't see the ocean until he was fifteen, but when he returned from the war he lived off it for the next twenty years as a deckhand, then a second mate, then a skipper. Until his wife died of influenza, and he was stuck with Lee's infant father, and he took Jack Southern out to the goldfields to meet his grandfather, only to discover old Donal's bones scattered round the campsite by wild dogs, and dragged up onto the rock by the giant monitor lizards whose noses were tuned to the scent of carrion. It was Lee's father who found Donal's skull, picked clean except for the odd scrap of red hair, beside the old soak in the dried-up riverbed where Lee had just shot the kangaroo. The skull had been scratched and clawed but there was a clean bullet hole in the roof with matchstick splinters on the outside. That told Grandpa Vernon how old Donal had been shot from beneath his face, and that the death was likely self-inflicted. Donal was a bushman and there was no chance someone had sprung him. The old man always said that he was going to shoot himself when the time was right. The country demanded it, he said. It was a tough and beautiful country and he had watched the seasons come and go and the animals and birds live and die. He had been a convict slave but would die a free man. Vernon and Lee's father gathered up what bones they could find and buried him next to his wife, beneath another cairn made of red granite sheeting.

*

Lee's father was busy dusting off his swag and getting ready to lie down for the night. The best part of the acid, he always said, was lying on your back in the clearing looking up at the night sky and the blazing stars and understanding your place in the meaningless realm. The thought that he was as insignificant as a speck of dust was a comfort to him, although Lee hadn't yet made peace with his inevitable fate. He angled his head in the direction of the giant red rock, silent and looming in the darkness. His father squinted, but nodded. Lee took off his shirt and his boots and without a torch padded off on the dusty path toward the rock. The moon hadn't risen, and outside of the firelight it was so dark that he couldn't see his hand. The dirt beneath his feet turned to rock, warm where the granite held the day's sun. The rock sloped upwards and his eyes adjusted to the dark and the rough granite held the grip of his feet. He walked with his hands ready to take his weight if he fell into one of the namma holes that were dry and papered with dead moss. The stars so bright that they hurt his eyes, the dark slope rising to a rounded peak that he sat upon, and looked to the horizon east where the moon would soon rise.

He kept his eyes open and senses keen. The air on his skin was cool as the desert cooled, the rock beneath his arse and legs warm. He tried to concentrate on the sounds of the desert woodland where herds of goat were followed by wild dogs, and where rabbit, camel, fox, donkey, wildcat and boar searched for food in the dark. Kangaroo, emu and snake. Spider and poisonous centipede. The birds asleep in their roosts: swallow and zebra finch and budgerigar, chitty-chitty, raven, black kite and wedge-tailed eagle.

As he often did when he was alone, Lee thought of his mother, who he barely remembered. A boy raised by wolves, Mrs Doyle, one of his teachers, had once muttered when Lee's father and his fellow Knights picked him up from school in their dirt bikes and Landies, dressed in army surplus camo gear and amped on speed for weekend exercises in the desert.

Lee didn't know much about his mother, and what little he knew had taken fifteen years of dragging out of his father. That her name was Mandy. That she liked to read, and taught

Lee to read. The story of his father taking her from her Mullewa home. Their weekends along the coast, surfing the remote breaks. That she liked The Rolling Stones. Her beauty. How she'd waited for Jack Southern when he volunteered for Vietnam in '68 – his training up in Queensland and then his twelve-month tour with the 3 RAR. A month back in Geraldton before training with the SAS, and then the second tour. She waited nearly three years and wrote to him and sent him pictures. Twenty years old when Lee was born. Then everything went wrong after Lee's birth. A kind of sadness came over her that she couldn't shake. Was a bad mother. Left Lee in his filth. Stopped looking after herself, too. Didn't understand what Lee's father was about, with his veteran friends and their weekends in the desert. Lacked political consciousness. Lacked ambition. Respect, and self-respect. Drank cheap goon wine from sun-up. Then one day Lee's father came home from work at the panelbeaters and she was gone. No note. Nothing packed. Just gone.

There was nothing of his mother left in their house except a few paperbacks. Lee found them by accident in a bag of fishing gear. He knew that they were hers because she'd written her name on the front cover in red pen. Heinlein's *Stranger in a Strange Land*. Dick's *Do Androids Dream of Electric Sheep?* Ursula K. Le Guin's *City of Illusions*. He read and reread them countless times, trying to get a picture of what kind of woman she was. The Ursula K. Le Guin novel was a library book, and when Lee was fourteen he went to the Geraldton library and asked the librarian, an old woman with sharp eyes, if she remembered his mother. Despite the decade that'd passed since her disappearance, the librarian did remember because they'd often chatted when Lee's father was away. She seemed lonely, the old woman told him. She liked science fiction but also writers like Jack Kerouac and Kurt Vonnegut. Thomas Pynchon. Hermann Hesse. Richard Brautigan. Iris Murdoch. Then, on the librarian's recommendation: Simone de Beauvoir, Sylvia Plath, Maya Angelou, Doris Lessing – all ordered from Perth libraries. Lee wrote the names down as fast as the librarian recited them before she took the page and corrected his spelling. He spent the next year reading everything his mother had read, but in secret, because he didn't want his father to know. Lee's father wouldn't have allowed any of the books in the house, seeing them as distractions from the ten or so books that he pored over and asked Lee to read to him.

Lee looked over the dark moonscape of the rock and the quiet desert woodland and the moon rising over the horizon. It was like he was on another planet. He lit a cigarette and felt the weight of the dome of rock that was mostly hidden beneath the red dirt like an iceberg in the ocean, and he on the top of it, and he saw precisely the shape of the rock beneath the ground. From his position, the forest appeared thick to the horizon, when in fact the ancient quondong, sandalwood and mallee trees were spaced like they'd been planted by a careful gardener. This was an ancient land that was patient during the day under the sun that had weathered the rocks and shaped the trees that were spindly and tough. Where the apex predators were dark-skinned reptiles and dark-feathered eagles that had lived since the time of the dinosaurs, so that Lee felt like a pale hologram placed temporarily in the world. Even so, the blush of love he felt for the land flooded his heart with a purity of understanding and appreciation. He felt the same swelling of love for his father who'd placed him there for the very purpose.

7.

Lee struck out at the touch on his forehead, rolling before he was awake. He hit the wall on the other side of the bed. He blinked, his heart racing, the room dark. He crawled over the sheets and flicked on the lamp. It was Francesca, kneeling and rocking while holding her head. He knew what he'd done, and touched her shoulder, which was the wrong thing to do. She flinched, and struck out herself.

'Get away from me, psycho.' She sat on her haunches and held the side of her face. 'I was just going to take your temperature. You'd thrown off all the blankets. You were thrashing about, grinding your teeth. I thought you might've got an infection.'

Lee dropped his legs over the mattress, looked into her eyes. 'Sorry. I got a habit of doing that. My father wakes me with the point of his foot.'

Frankie dabbed at her temple and looked at her fingers. There was no blood. 'You threw me into the wall. While you were asleep. Your eyes were closed.'

Lee didn't answer. She offered him her hand, and he drew her up. There wasn't much space between the bed and the wall and she smelled of soap and sweat. He let go of her hand, and backed up so that she could move. She was dressed in a white singlet and green scrub pants.

'Thanks for checking in on me.'

'It's nothing.'

Frankie looked at her watch, then at Lee. 'Come with me for a sec.'

He followed her through the empty house and into her room. She sat on her bed and patted beside her. On the bedside table was a saucer, a syringe and a glass of water.

'What's that?'

'A little painkiller to see you through.'

She drew out a small paper packet from beneath her pillow.

'I'm good,' he said, but didn't leave.

She tapped out a mound of powder onto the saucer, refolded the packet and drew up some water from the glass with the syringe, which she dribbled into the powder. 'Don't worry, this is a fresh work. I'm a nurse and I don't share. See enough hep cases every day. You want to avoid those interferon treatments if you can.'

She took out the plunger nub of the syringe and mixed the water until the powder dissolved. Removed a cigarette from her packet and broke off a filter, then split it in half with her thumbnail. She dropped the filter into the saucer and replaced the plunger into the syringe. She drew up the liquid and tapped it, gave a little squirt and tapped it again.

'I said sit down.'

There was a darkening bruise on her temple where he'd struck her, and he sat. It didn't take long for her to find a vein in the crux of his arm. She drew back blood and sent the plunger home. She removed the needle and placed some tissue over the little thorn of blood.

It was more of the same; that sweet body warmth but coming on fast. He felt himself sink into the bed as his muscles relaxed, even though he felt lighter than air.

'Thanks,' he grunted.

She glanced at her watch again and then there was a look in her eye. She stared at him and her toughness was gone, replaced by a wistful concern, or was it guilt?

'What?' he asked, but she shook her head.

They both heard the throaty reverberation of a V8 in the street, trembling the windowpane as it pulled into the drive. Frankie gathered up the makings and swept them into the drawer. She stood and left him alone in the room. He tried to stand but his feet were moulded to the floor. There were boot-steps on the front porch and the screen slammed open. Lee watched four men in donkey jackets wearing balaclavas pass down the hall. Kinslow entered and saw him.

'He's in here,' was all he said. Took a step into the room and launched an underhand right into Lee's gut. Put two hands on Lee's shoulders and fixed a boot on his groin, holding him down. Lee tried to shrug the hands off but the four men swarmed him. One of them lifted up a dark sack and slung it over his head. That smell of ether again. He remembered the look in Frankie's eyes and knew.

*

The smack in Lee's blood helped. He didn't know how long he'd sat in the chair, his hands bound. Through the heavy black cotton he could see light above his head and the room smelled of dust and he understood that he was in a cellar cut into substrate limestone. He remembered snatches of consciousness before he was dragged down into the cellar. The smell of jasmine blossoms in the yard, and Brasso inside the house that echoed with boot-steps.

The floor beneath his bare feet was unpolished concrete slab. There was no sound of traffic and no noise except for the boot-steps on floorboards above his head, and then the creaking of a door opening and men walking down wooden stairs.

The room wasn't big. The sound of their moving around him was close, and their smells were strong. Old Spice deodorant, oil and wet wool. He didn't remember rain. The smell of stale tobacco.

There were several other men in the room but nobody spoke and they'd ceased moving. Lee wasn't going to speak. The obvious scenario was that Kinslow planned to hand him over to the Knights, for guns or money. If so, he'd soon be in the boot of a car headed north to Geraldton, to be buried in a shallow grave alongside his father.

The men's silence was odd, and he imagined how he must look to them, sacked, bound and barefoot, awaiting his end.

Then new footsteps on the stairs, hesitant and uneven, the creaking sound of weight on a balustrade. A thin sound preceding the footsteps, a walking stick.

It was the same hesitant step that he remembered from the motel room, when he was last bound to a chair. It was the old man. As soon as the shuffling stopped before him, Lee spoke.

'You again.'

This gave the old man pause, because he stopped moving and said nothing.

'You going to take this sack off my head? I've seen how you run your outfit. It's a bit embarrassing, isn't it?'

The old man laughed, but didn't reply.

'I told you I don't know my father's weapons guy, and there's nothing I can do to help.'

'Oh, but there is, *boy*, there is.'

The old man's voice, calm and assured, used to being listened to. He tapped his cane on the ground, waited. 'We could hand you over to your father's remnant party. They've put word out that they'll pay well for you. But that isn't my style. You have value to us. Potentially.'

Lee waited. The silence was designed to draw it out of him, but he resisted. Finally, the old man spoke. 'Don't you have any questions?'

'My father told me about people like you. Toy soldiers and fantasists.'

'You've never had to think for yourself, have you?'

Lee kept quiet. It was true.

'In fact, we are, most of us, ex-soldiers,' the old man said. 'What we believe, we learned the hard way. That the yellow man is no lesser a creature than the white man except for the fact that he has a higher toleration for slavery. For following the herd. The yellow man desires everything to be harmonious and will tolerate things that no white man can tolerate. But restless and rebellious and easily bored with harmony are we.'

'I don't mind hearing your lecture, mister, but I feel like a dickhead talking through this sack.'

The old man chortled again. 'You are a case in point, young man, but I'm afraid that removing the impediment isn't possible. Nor will you ever see my face. We don't operate like that. Please don't think of yourself as a prisoner or a penitent in a hood, but rather as a falcon whose eyes have been covered prior to a hunting expedition.'

'Let me guess, you're a big-wheel businessman.'

There was an awkward silence, a scraping of boots. Lee could almost see the old man shake his head as another of them raised his fists.

'I am not like your father, that is true. We differ in important ways. He is essentially a survivalist, but we don't believe that the end will come suddenly. There will be no invasion. What we'll see is more of the same. The racial dilution of white nations. A slow genocide, but a genocide all the same. We seek to intervene now, where we can, and bring about our cultural renaissance.'

'Where am I?'

The old man sighed. 'I'm not going to bargain with you, Lee, or waste any further time. I'm going to give you a choice that sounds like an ultimatum. You are precisely what we're looking for. We are under surveillance and our broader organisations have been infiltrated by state actors. You will have nothing to do with Kinslow's thugs or their antics. You will not participate in any of their actions or attend any rallies. You will receive orders and report to me alone, by way of a trusted intermediary. You are trained for warfare and you're a cleanskin as far as ASIO is concerned. You've shown your courage and training. But, and I advise you to answer honestly, have you ever killed a man?'

He was serious. His voice in Lee's ear now. The smell of sherry on his breath. Cologne on his clothes.

'No, I haven't.'

'Have you ever seen a dead man, taken violently?'

Lee's training and common sense required him to answer no, but he was tired and wanted this charade to end. The truth, then. 'Yes, I have.'

The image of Emma's cousin, David, hanging from the winch of the prawn trawler, two fingers of one hand trapped inside the noose. The bulging eyes and purple tongue, face the colour of blood. For six hours David had hung there. The coroner ruled suicide but it was no suicide and everyone in town knew. Including Emma, the reason she'd left him, and Geraldton behind.

'You're still a boy, but I can see in you the proud white man you'll become. I want to apologise for the beatings that you've suffered in the course of your journey to this place, and this point in time.'

'What if I say no?'

'What, indeed? We need funds to pursue our ambitions in ways legal and extrajudicial. You are worth something to the Knights' leadership. You will be handed over to them, as they have asked, dead or alive.'

As though to emphasise his point, Lee heard the unmistakable click of a round being chambered into a handgun.

'But I don't think that you'll say no. Not when you hear what I have to say. I think you'll be most eager to work with us.'

'Say it then.'

'Your father. He isn't dead. Far from it – he is alive and well, even if … inaccessible. And before you ask how this might be proven, I will tell you that we can prove it. He is in custody, in a secure facility. He has been charged with a minor drug offence, but he's also in witness protection.'

It took a few second for that to sink in. 'You're lying. My father's no dog. And there hasn't been anything in the papers. He vanished after Brady Downs' murder. Downs' brother killed him. He wouldn't just leave me –'

'All in good time, Lee. Now, what is your decision?'

The old man stepped away. Another man, wearing boots, stepped into his place. Lee could smell the gun oil. Feel the cold black eye of the pistol barrel trained on his spine, where his neck entered his skull. Quick, painless and near bloodless.

The words he had learned, and that he dearly believed.

The only free man is the man who doesn't care.

But he nodded, and his head was gripped, and then the smell of ether.

8.

It was the pain in his head that awoke him, and the glass of water someone tossed onto his face. Lee focused on the plasterwork around the ceiling. Little curlicues of flowers and vine, painted white.

It hurt to raise his neck. His skull felt like it'd been scoured out with steel wool. His eyes burned.

It was Robbie, standing above him. 'Get dressed, Lee. I'm riding with you today. Kinslow said it. Your face like it is, working on your own, you'll scare the punters.'

Robbie left the room, dressed in his True West Towing service uniform of shirt, trousers and boots. Was he one of the silent men last night in the old man's cellar? Lee didn't think so. There had been something unnatural about their silence throughout. Like the old man said: military trained.

There was a pot of filtered coffee on the heating element in the kitchen. Lee had slept in his jeans. Someone had taken off his shirt. He looked about the house for Frankie, but she wasn't there. Instead, Robbie was in her room, looking through her laundry basket, running his fingers through her silken knickers. Their eyes met and Robbie laughed, held the knickers up to his nose and took a long noisy sniff.

Lee went to the kitchen and drank his coffee. There were no painkillers in the house that he could find. He dressed in his room, looking at his face, wincing every time he turned his neck. That pulpy look around his cheekbones and mouth was fading, although his nose and eyes were still blackened.

Robbie was snorting a line of speed off the formica kitchen table. He held up the rolled ten-dollar note, and Lee shook his head.

'I took you for a goey-man,' Robbie said, 'intense as you are. Suit yourself. I like to get primed for the road. Let's go.'

Lee's truck was parked in the drive. There were True West Towing decals on the front and rear windows, and magnetic signs on both doors. Robbie climbed into the passenger seat and passed Lee a folded piece of paper. 'You're now a licensed tow-truck driver, insured through us in case you damage one of the mugs' vehicles. From now on you can fill up at the depot, where we'll meet every day, at eight. I've been told not to come round here anymore.'

There was a question in Robbie's eyes, and a deeper envy. Lee privy to something that Robbie wasn't.

The Ford started with a throaty roar as Lee engaged reverse, pulled back over the drive and rolled onto the street. He put her in first, but didn't lift the clutch. 'You don't need to babysit me. You want me to drop you at the depot?'

Robbie looked thwarted in some way. 'I'm acting on

orders … Just like you. I go back to the depot alone, Kinslow's gonna freak.'

That question in his eyes again, hoping that Lee would share. Instead, Lee nodded. 'Alright, where the fuck are we? And which way do I go?'

Lee's helplessness seemed to appease Robbie, and he laughed. 'We're in Inglewood, north of the city. Take a left toward Beaufort Street. Turn right there.'

They drove down the quiet suburban street of bungalows and weatherboards until they hit the busier road. At the corner, on the stop signs, on the rubbish bins and on a steel-grey electricity exchange box were plastered posters.

Asians Out. Every Job for an Asian is a Job LOST to a White.

Jews make up 50% of the richest 1%.

The Holocaust is a LIE.

Robbie was grinning from ear to ear. He nodded to turn right and Lee pulled into the morning traffic, moving off the higher ground toward the city glimmering in the distance. On every bin, street sign and bus stop were the same posters. Hundreds of them among the people going about their business, the newsagents and delis, the sandwich bars, real estate agents and pubs.

'Slow down, right … here.'

Lee looked to where Robbie was furtively pointing across the truck. Furtive because of the two paddy-wagons on the footpath. Three coppers leaning on the bonnet, looking out over the traffic. Behind them was a burnt-out shopfront, the glass windows shattered across the pavement. The sign above the burnt awning read 'Hop Sing Chinese Restaurant.' The inside charred and caved in, water-soaked.

On the corner two tall young Asian men comforted an older woman in an ankle-length coat, her face hidden but her shoulders trembling. Beside them an old Chinese man stared into the traffic, stunned, nothing in his expression. Robbie wound down the passenger window, started rubbing his fists in his eyes, the universal boohoo gesture. The young men stiffened and watched them pass, their faces a mask of hatred.

'Oh, fuck me,' said Robbie. 'That's beautiful. Wish I had a camera. Show and tell tonight at the debrief.'

'Tell me how you did it,' Lee said.

The traffic opened up in the right lane and Lee rolled the Ford down into Mount Lawley. Robbie took his time answering, but finally couldn't help himself. 'There was a busted eave. We got a weed-sprayer and hosed petrol into the roof. Forced a back door and doused everything. Final thing, we smashed the front window and tossed in a Molotov. *Wwhhhooooshh! Bang!* No more chogie restaurant in *our* neighbourhood.'

Lee got the Ford out from behind a bus and turned onto Vincent Street. 'I guess you chose it because it was a standalone building,' he said.

'Very observant. Yeah. We don't want to be burning down any Aussie businesses.'

In the park to their left was a mob of blackfellas, gathered under the reaching arms of a Moreton Bay fig, wearing beanies and heavy flannel. In the cool morning air the dampness rose off the cut grass and surface of the lake, whose edges were retained with brickwork.

'What's this park called?' Lee asked.

Robbie sniffed, looked around for a sign. 'I don't know. Coon Park? It's always full of 'em. We have our sport sometimes. Give 'em some of this.'

Robbie smacked his fist into his other hand, but Lee didn't believe him. He knew how handy the average blackfella was; male or female, old or young.

'Did this used to be wetlands? Smells like it.'

Robbie laughed. 'That's not the lake you're smelling, mate.'

Lee didn't comment any more. He'd meant the dampness and tannic smell, the unlikely presence of so much water on higher ground, meaning an underground spring or watercourse.

'Let's get on the freeway and see what we see. Hope your first day on the job isn't like mine was.'

Lee lit a cigarette and offered one to Robbie, who shook his head. Robbie was waiting for Lee to ask him about his first day, and when he didn't, took a deep breath. 'Mate, no shit, my *first day*! I was riding with Kinslow, over on Leach Highway. We heard the coppers on the UHF. Got there in a jiffy, even before the coppers. It was at the lights in Booragoon. Fucken peak-hour traffic. Some motorcyclist had come across the bonnet of a little Jap-crap Camry or something like it. The bike was in the intersection. The rider's body was snapped around a light pole. No shit, the Camry driver, little bloke in a suit, looked like a schoolteacher or something. He was out in the intersection kicking something around, raving like a spastic. Kinslow just said, "Oh fuck," and I looked closer. The motorbike rider had lost his head. The schoolteacher was out in the intersection, kicking around the helmet, the poor bastard's head still inside it. He was kickin it around like a soccer ball, and shoutin at it, kickin and shoutin, the head rolling all over the place. The bloke was in shock, see – didn't even know what he was doin. I held him by the shoulders while Kinslow give him a little tap on the chin, just to settle him down. Then he started throwin up and weepin. Fuck me. The coppers arrived and I had to go get the head, just so traffic could resume. Carried it in the helmet. Just the stump of his neck showin, the visor still down. Fucken sick, mate, what you see in this job sometimes.'

Perhaps it was the speed, but the pitch of Robbie's voice kept rising as the excitement of describing the experience built. 'Mate, I think I will have one of those cigarettes.' Robbie's hands were shaking as he lit up, blowing smoke out into the morning traffic. 'You don't talk much, Lee, do you?'

It was an accusation, and Lee didn't acknowledge it, turning south onto the freeway. He tuned the UHF as he drove. There were some things he needed to know, however. 'What are the police codes for the different call-outs?'

'Not as smart as you think, are ya?'

'Guess not.'

Lee only had to wait, and pretty soon Robbie began his training spiel. Lee listened intently, because it was what he needed to know. When Robbie was finished, he added, 'You don't look like a Nazi.'

Lee shook his head, spat out the window.

'Something funny, smart boy?'

This was how it was going to be, all day. Robbie needling him, hoping for a reaction.

'I'm not a Nazi.'

'Then what the fuck is Kinslow interested in you for?'

'I'm a prospect, was a prospect, in the Knights. My father started it, back in the seventies, when he got back from Vietnam.'

'Sounds like a bikie gang. Kinslow told me it's called The White Knights.'

'Used to be. Not anymore.'

'White Knights, as in … noble and pure?'

'Kind of the opposite. It's supposed to be ironic.'

Unusually, Robbie didn't reply. Lee looked at him. Robbie didn't understand.

'You mean, like sarcastic?'

'Yeah, like sarcastic.'

Robbie was an open book. In between changing lanes, Lee looked at him again. Could anticipate the next question. Thought about what he'd say. How the Knights started as a bikie gang, made up initially of Vietnam veterans, still had the chain-of-command of a bikie gang. Funded their operations through selling drugs and guns, like a bikie gang. Were feared around town, just like a bikie gang. Had 'good mates' in the local coppers and among the guards at Greenough Prison, too. Their clubhouse the gun range. Recruiting only through the original families.

'Your father was the president.'

'Yeah, he was.'

'And now he's dead.'

Lee met Robbie's eyes, which were smug.

'*Kinslow* told me that too. Something about one of the other leaders, getting found buried in the sand dunes behind your house. Your father did it. Then he got payback.'

Lee ignored him. He understood now why Kinslow wasn't in the room last night, with the old man and the others. The last thing Lee had heard, before the ether threw him backwards off a cliff, was the old man saying that Kinslow could come in now. His job just to deliver Lee to them, and take him back to the house. Run the tow trucks. Be the public face.

'You don't like me much, do you?'

Another goad. The antagonism in character, looking for weakness.

'Kinslow also told me that your gang might've knocked off a bloke running for Geraldton mayor. That true? Cos he was makin noises about dope plantations in the area. The cops bein too friendly with organised crime figures? That kind of thing. Why would Kinslow say that if it weren't true?'

'You believe everything he says?'

Robbie snorted. 'But you're just a prospect. You wouldn't take a hand in anything like that. Still, you reckon you're better than us, that's pretty obvious.'

What Robbie said about Lee being a mere prospect was

true. Most of the things that the Knights were notorious for had taken place when Lee was a child. Like the time a Korean sailor had allegedly raped a local girl, whose father took it to the Knights, and not the coppers. Twenty armed Knights, led by Lee's father, had taken over the ship at port, placed a guard on the gangway. According to the legend, they bashed every member of the crew, then invited the girl's father on board to lay into the rapist. Then they set charges in the ship's hold and blew out its side, before setting it on fire. The wreck was still there on one of the local beaches, where it was dragged and dumped after sinking. None of the sailors had reported what happened, claiming injuries after the explosion. They flew home minus one crew member, whose charred body was found after the blaze.

Or the time one of the local coppers came to the Knights with a problem. Up in Broome, some of the dope and speed dealing had been taken over by members of a NSW bikie gang, went by the name of the Fangs. They even went so far as to start wearing their patches around town, scaring the tourists and setting up a clubhouse. The local sergeant didn't want it known in the city that he'd lost control of the situation, would be bad for his career. Could the Knights help? Lee's father and ten others packed their gear into Land Rovers and headed north. They kidnapped the ringleader and held him out in the desert. They made a time and place for the exchange. It was a trap and an opportunity for some live-fire training. They ambushed the bikies with heavy automatic fire, killed them all and buried them deep. Sent the severed head of the leader, packed in dry ice, to the club headquarters in Bankstown.

Stories like this, and more. Lee had grown up with them, heard them recited in the schoolyard by the other kids, behind his back. He didn't know if any of them were true, except that his father never talked about them. His father liked telling stories, but would never talk about crimes that were true, even to his son.

The traffic on the Narrows Bridge was heavy, and Lee scanned the emergency lanes in both directions, the river opening up wide and shallow.

'You don't want to be part of the movement we got goin, that's fine with me. Only room for true believers at the pointy end of the spear.'

Lee thought about answering with a question, but he couldn't be bothered. He'd grown up in a largely white town, and had never seen much evidence of the so-called superiority of his own race.

Robbie was a good example.

'You've seen what we're doing. We can't advertise in the papers. Jew money means no newspaper or radio or TV station will take our advertising dollar. So we win the propaganda war on the streets. Just because there aren't many of us, doesn't mean shit. We've got the heart. The coppers and ASIO are already lookin at us, and I say that with pride …'

The pain in Lee's head wasn't getting any better. He took his sunglasses off the dash and put them on. There were pelicans on each of the light-posts that straddled Canning Bridge, and he admired their symmetry: the giant forms, pink gullets and intelligent eyes trained on the river south, waiting for a school of mullet to break the surface. The broth-coloured water lapped at the sandy shore, sedge and reed-banks rising up to the steel barriers of the freeway. There were a couple of joggers and cyclists moving over the path. An old man wading and casting for flathead on a submerged sandbank. A couple leaning into one another, seated on a park bench. Normal life, and all of it alien to him.

If Lee kept to the freeway he'd end up on a coast road to Bunbury, and from there it was coastal town to coastal town, right until the Nullarbor. He could start again, somewhere east. He had petrol money for a few days, and could take on paying work the rest of the way.

But what if it was true that his father was alive, somewhere in the city?

Despite what Lee felt when he looked at civilians going about their day-to-day – the yearning for a life of his own – his father was all that Lee had.

'Those Knights that killed your father. They know where you are and what you're doing?'

The smugness was back in Robbie's voice, helping himself to another cigarette, looking down the freeway and everywhere but Lee.

Lee turned the Ford onto Leach Highway, into the suburbs. If Robbie wondered where they were going, he said nothing. He was flicking through the tapes in the glove box.

'We got to get you away from this metal shit. There's some good local bands. White pride and plenty of piss an' vinegar.

You're not jacked off at me, are ya? And where you headed? This way lies Fremantle. Freo Rocks turf. They see me down there I'll get scalped. Those wog boys are mean with a knife.'

Lee looked for a deli on one of the side streets. He needed an iced coffee or some black aspro. He noticed parked cars and recognised the gabled roofline of the standard shopfront. Robbie was still talking when Lee pulled up, palming the wheel into a park.

'You get me something? How 'bout a White Knight? Nah, just jokin. Get me a sausage roll and sauce?'

Lee nodded and tapped his pockets, the fold of cash still there.

Beside the front door, angling his face into the sunshine, was a black guy in his teens, seated on the footpath nursing a can of Fanta and an unlit cigarette. Black jeans and a sleeveless East Perth footy jumper, long curly hair, barefoot. He didn't look at Lee, who went inside the flystrip curtain doorway and straight to the fridge. He took a litre of iced coffee and pressed it to his forehead, then opened it and drank half of it down.

'Hey. No.'

A thin voice from the front of the store. Over the top of the aisle laid with titty magazines, greeting cards and newspapers, an old Chinese woman waggled her finger at him. Lee finished the iced coffee and took out some cold Mars bars, another litre of iced coffee. He made his way around the aisles and put the empty and the full on the counter. Lee was a good foot taller than the old lady, and he looked down onto her pale scalp and grey roots as she made his change. Despite the damage to his face she wasn't scared of him. She offered his coins and smiled, even met his eyes. 'Sorry. We get some bad customer. They steal.'

'Fair enough. No worries.'

The pie warmer contained the usual. He thanked the old lady and went out into the sun, peeling himself a Mars bar. He felt better already as the coffee, sugar and milk hit his stomach. He was tossing the empty carton into the nearest bin when he heard a sound behind him. He'd forgotten about the black kid in the footy jumper, who was right in his face, holding up a cigarette.

'Nummery wa?'

'What?'

'You gotta light for me nummery?'

Lee stepped back. The guy smelled like campfire smoke. His bloodshot eyes were warm and brown.

'You got a light, cuz?'

'It's in the truck.'

But the bloke didn't get out of his way. Instead of moving, he lifted his chin and pursed his lips, a question. Put a hand on Lee's chest, to stop him moving. 'Where your people from?'

'What?'

'I said, where your people from? What your country?'

The anger was sudden and powerful. With his free hand, Lee made an elbow and shoved it into the guy's chest, pushed him back a few steps. 'The fuck away from me.'

The guy backed up, but dropped his hands, rocked on the balls of his bare feet, the classic stance. Lee didn't move, but kept his right fist closed, ready to throw a southpaw jab.

A single word would bring it on, but Lee didn't want it. The last thing he wanted. He was sick of it.

He walked to the truck, ignoring the eyes of the other man, watching him leave. Lee climbed into the truck and turned the key. Robbie slapped him hard on the neck.

'Fucken nice one man. I think the boong might've pissed himself. You got my sausage roll?'

Lee released the handbrake. 'Nope. Forgot. You still want one?'

'Fucken oath I want one. Let's see if the boong's got anything left.'

Robbie got down from the cab. Lee waited until Robbie was inside the deli. He put the Ford in reverse and pulled onto the road, changed forward and drove off. The street was pruned bottlebrush and peppermint trees right to the highway. He got to the intersection and saw Robbie standing back there, in the middle of the road, his hands up and his mouth stuffed with pastry and meat.

9.

Lee found the address listed on Emma's letter. It was on another suburban street lined with peppermint trees, further west, sloping down toward the river. A two-storey pale brick affair with a skillion roof built over an excavated garage. Big windows to take in the view. Emma's father was a school principal and on a good salary.

It was the middle of the day and there was nobody around. Lee scanned the windows on the top floor and wondered which of the rooms was hers. Probably the one with the closed drapes and the little balcony. He looked at the house and figured out the best way to scale the wall and reach her room, as he used to do back in Geraldton. She had once told him about boys in alpine Austria risking their lives by climbing to the top of mountains to pick a single edelweiss flower as proof of their love.

Lee'd been with Emma in the back of his father's Sandman, the rear doors open to a view of the ocean. Lee had tried to think of an equivalent gesture of romantic bravery that didn't involve fighting, or crime, or drag racing, and that was the problem with his hometown right there.

He had already told her about spearfishing with his father off the back reefs, drawing in tiger sharks with fish-heads tied to his belt, his heart blooming inside his chest like a jellyfish while his father trod water beside him. Lee hoping for a juvenile tiger shark and not a school of bronze whalers. The shotgun cartridge loaded into the bang-stick held in his shaking hands. A shark's brain about the size of his big toe. Miss it and it'd just make the shark angry. His father similarly armed beside him, looking into the deep blue depths that sloped down to the continental shelf. The ten-foot tiger emerging from the gloom with slow swipes of its tail, moving to circle them, taking a look with its cold eye – the tiger stripes a nice camouflage in the dappled sunlight near the surface. It came closer and Lee's heart pounded and his bladder emptied and the thing was moving impossibly fast, his father gone from beside him, a glance telling Lee that he was now hunting his own shark, far bigger and more wary, thirty feet to his left. Lee hung at the surface, trying to make himself limp, knowing that the shark could read his heart, could smell the chemicals of fear on his skin and the piss that was leaking from his wetsuit in warm threads.

He hung limp, and waited, terrified that his forced calmness had become paralysis, turning the bang-stick in his hands to prove that he was alive but scared that he'd drop it. Surf crashed onto the reef a hundred metres behind him. Sunlight danced on his head. The shark feint-charged and looped back around. Lee heard the drowned percussion of his father's bang-stick discharging, looked over to see the second giant tiger swimming erratically then thrashing, and then stopping all movement, gliding down into the blue depths. Lee turned his head and his own tiger was sweeping past him again, a closer orbit, and Lee took a breath and kicked and slammed the stick into the shark's head, just behind the eyes. He felt the cartridge detonate and the shockwave pulse up his arms and into his shoulders as the pig-shot burst under the animal's skin. The shark looked at him a moment, juddered and shivered, rolled its eyes, jawing the water. It tried to swim but merely spun, a slow death spiral, circling down into the gloom. Lee watched it and felt terror and pity, his father's hands on his arm, pulling him back to the surface for air.

The story didn't impress Emma. She ran her hand over his face, looking into his eyes. 'Your eyes are so sad,' she said, and held him tight, squeezing and releasing. She felt sorry for him, and he understood that her pity was because of the life that his father demanded of him, and for the first time Lee felt anger toward his father, and resentment too.

*

A police van entered the street at the bottom of the hill and Lee realised that he'd been sitting in the truck staring at the house for some time. He lifted the book of maps off the seat beside him and began to scan the nearby streets for her school. The police car passed, the hatless driver ducking under the sun visor to check Lee out. This was a rich neighbourhood and neither Lee nor his truck fitted the picture of quiet streets, manicured gardens and fancy houses.

Emma hadn't named her school. There were a couple of private colleges in the area, but only one of them was Catholic. He dog-eared the page and drove to the end of the street, turned in the general north-east direction indicated on the map. The school wasn't far away and he hoped that it was the right one. It was close enough for her to walk. He could park up one day soon, when his face was less disfigured. Wait for her by the side of the road.

There were girls of all ages on the sports fields, the youngest ones playing chasey and the older ones practising netball in bloomers and t-shirts. Groups of girls sat in lazy circles under trees with a view over the river, but their uniform wasn't the one that Emma had described, and Lee searched through the grids across the suburbs toward Fremantle, and north of the river, where there were several that sounded Catholic enough. He drove the truck down Stirling Highway across the river that narrowed toward the port busy with container ships, the hot stink of live sheep transports carried on the sea breeze. He found Maria College just as the siren sounded to end lunchtime. Girls wearing the uniform described by Emma moved in clots toward the largest buildings. He drove the truck closer to the river, looking for the place where girls who smoked would gather outside the cyclone fenceline, but couldn't see anywhere likely.

The school grounds were deserted and he put the Ford in gear and followed the river through a new suburb and then a light industrial area back toward the port. His plan was to go to the harbour, past the gigantic crane derricks and sit on the limestone groyne at South Mole, where he and his father had always eaten Cicerello's fish and chips.

He crossed Stirling Bridge but got boxed between an empty sheep truck and a two-container road train, and had to follow them deeper into suburban Fremantle. At the first opportunity he headed toward the limestone ridgeline that glinted with sunlight and rose over the city below. He was nearly at the peak of the hill when the traffic thickened. He saw a woman standing beside her Holden with the bonnet popped while another man who'd parked his ute on the verge attached jump leads to his own car. Lee's Ford wouldn't be needed, and he joined the right lane and had gone about a hundred metres when the traffic slowed and he watched two thickset men skipping on the pavement while another shadow-boxed. There were no signs, but Lee pulled over and parked the truck. Two more men ran out from a sunken driveway that led beneath a video store.

Lee turned off the ignition and locked the truck, then walked up to the men on the pavement. None of them showed any interest, and he looked down the driveway to a parking lot at the rear of the building. He walked down the steep drive and heard the familiar sound of gloves hitting bags and sharp exhalations and the clinking of weights. Behind the corner was a darkened room with a bare concrete floor and heavy bags bolted to frames in the concrete ceiling. A thin young man at the back of the room moved through his circuit, turning to work the speedballs, the heavy bag beside him still creaking and rocking. The room smelled of stale sweat and Dencorub. There was a boxing ring in the farthest corner with a carpet floor. The ceiling was low and the room was hot.

The gym was exactly what he'd been looking for. Lee glanced around and noticed the older man who'd been watching him the whole time. He was tidying up a shelf of gloves that he'd pulled to the floor to sort out in pairs. He was black-skinned and dressed in stubbies and a tight singlet over a gut shaped like a basketball. He waved Lee into the room. As Lee got closer he could see that the old blackfella was a good size, with long arms and large hands. He smiled at Lee and shouted, 'Frank!'

From an office to Lee's right an older white man emerged, lean and rangy with combed wet hair, wiping his face with a towel. He was shirtless and dressed in footy shorts and thongs. He wiped his hands and reached out a paw for Lee to shake. 'I'm Frank. That's Gerry.'

They looked like a couple of ex-pugs and neither of them said anything about the state of Lee's face. He nodded. 'Lee.'

Frank waved a hand at the floor of the gym. 'Help yourself. If it works, let Gerry know. I've gotta go to work. See ya, mate.'

Frank went back into the office and shut the door. Gerry knelt to sort out the gloves. Lee untied his boots and slipped off his socks. He stood in his jeans, shirtless. The cement was oily underfoot and he went straight for the nearest heavy bag, banded around its guts with gaffer tape. He gave it a left jab to make sure it wasn't filled with sand. His ribs ached and his face felt like a papier-mâché mask but it was good to move.

'You don't want to wear gloves?'

Lee ignored Gerry behind him. Began to rock on his feet, warming up with a flurry of jabs, letting the impact of the blows loosen his shoulders. When he was ready he stood back and took the stance and belted the bag with five side kicks, his hands balanced above his head and his foot returning to the same mark on the floor. He was starting to sweat in the hot room and he wiped the balls of his feet on his jeans and repeated the kicks, this time with his left leg. The smacks on the leather were loud and satisfying. He stood back and delivered a kick–punch combination. He could feel his heart pumping faster and his skin begin to tingle. His face wasn't aching anymore as his body made its own painkillers and pumped them around his body.

'Hey.'

Lee turned and Gerry was holding up a pair of wraps. 'You don't have to wear gloves, but you got to wear wraps. I don't want your blood on my bags.'

Lee saw that he'd already skinned the two contact knuckles on each hand, which were seeping a clear fluid. Now he noticed the prison tattoos on the dark skin of the other man. Ink teardrops on his weathered face. His arms a mess of faded patterns that were indecipherable in the shadows.

Gerry passed the white bandages and went back to his business while Lee wrapped his hands. He worked the heavy bag for a couple of minutes before he noticed the black man watching him.

'Keep that left shoulder up.'

Lee hadn't sought the man's advice and pretended he hadn't heard. Next thing, he felt a whack on his back. It was Gerry, holding up a leather face mask with an iron grille. 'Yer face is messed up enough. You better wear this.'

Gerry walked over to the boxing ring and climbed inside, turned and waited for Lee to follow. Lee had never worn a mask before, but understood that it was a good idea. 'And get yourself sixteen-ounce gloves. We got carpet here, so your bare feet don't matter.'

Lee moved cautiously around the man, who turned with Lee's circle. There was nothing in his eyes except the job, scanning Lee's footwork. Lee made his first foray with a double jab and then a third jab to the stomach but the old man was surprisingly fast, ducking, dancing and circling round. Every time Lee entered the man's range he got a sharp tap on the forehead, the jabs deliberately north of his broken nose but powerful enough to snap his neck back. Lee went in with a flurry but the old man danced away, giving him another tap in the process. There was no enjoyment in his dark eyes, just the odd grunt for Lee to keep his left shoulder up, to keep moving. Now Gerry went on the offensive, forcing Lee back into the corners with repeated jabs, boxing him in, rounding his shoulders and protecting his face and taking the hooks to the top of his blunt head. The guy was a bull, and there was no let-up. Pretty soon they were bathed in sweat, Lee short of breath, his heart hammering and his knees weak, although the old guy showed no signs of fatigue and just kept bustling and jabbing.

Lee put up his hands. The disappointment on the man's face was obvious, although he nodded.

They stood in the sunlight and let the wind cool them, loosening their wraps. 'You show promise. We usually open early evening, for the local kids. You start coming regular I'll give you a key, so you can train whenever you want. We spar every night at seven if that's your thing.'

'What do I owe you?' Lee asked, only now getting his breath back, his face still full of blood.

Gerry shook his head. 'Nothin, mate. Till you start coming regular. Sling us a five every now and then.'

There was no warmth in his voice, and Lee understood. The man had seen something in Lee's eyes that he was used to seeing. It didn't require comment, until the look became words, or something else.

Lee was too hot to get back in his boots. He stood there, feeling like an idiot, holding his boots and socks, his t-shirt hooped around his neck. He waited until the black man looked up, and met his eye.

'Thanks,' he said, and the old guy nodded.

*

Lee followed the river toward the city, getting to know the smaller streets whose names he committed to memory. There were countless little bays where the river opened up to Melville

Water, separated by limestone cliffs and mansions with high walls. Down on the mudflats were weed-beds and patches of sedge-grass and reed. He could see different species of waders poking about in the shallows. Pelicans and shags stood in the sunshine watching the smaller birds fuss and preen. North across the river Lee saw a pod of five dolphins cruising the shallows, swimming laps around the pylons and buoys, playing rather than hunting. One of them was a baby and, as he'd done ever since his father taught him at Shark Bay, Lee felt like swimming out and joining them. He'd speak to them underwater, mimicking their sonar chatter of squeaks and bended notes. Instead, he turned the ignition and moved east and north toward the city, in no particular hurry, but examining the new feeling that had occupied his mind since leaving the boxing gym.

It had been there throughout the day, but now that the afternoon was drifting toward evening it was becoming obvious. The urge had no name because he'd never felt it before, except that every time the flush of anxiety grew in his stomach he thought of Frankie. Lee examined his mind for something to explain the recurring image of Frankie, but there was nothing there. It was his body speaking to him, trying to trick his mind. It wasn't Frankie that his body was yearning for but the peace that came with the little push of her syringe. The image of her crouched beside him crystallised with the force of understanding. The tenderness she'd shown him, and the warm shadows cast by her black hair over her eyes, and the touch of her fingers on his forearm had become the same thing as the flushing tranquil warmth, and the hours of wakeful dreaming that her syringe had delivered with its finest point and prick of steel.

Knowing this, not fighting it, Lee turned the Ford toward the freeway north, the sunlight warm on his knuckles and face as he joined the heavy traffic, barely noticing it over the rising expectation of seeing Frankie when he returned to the house in Inglewood. He didn't look at the burnt-out restaurant on Beaufort Street, or the hundreds of posters with their slogans and caricatures of Jews and Asians. Within the time it took to relive the memory of Frankie in her room, gently holding his forearm, he was there. He parked on the verge, noticing for the first time the twin frangipani trees that had grown above the height of the guttering, and whose white flowers with their sunburst yellow centres were angled into the sunlight. He pulled open the creaking flyscreen door and entered the cool dark hallway. Frankie was in her room, wiping her work-shoes with a spit-dabbed tissue, and she looked at him and nodded, then patted the bed alongside her.

10.

The disapproving look on the man's face told Lee that he was military, casting his eyes over the messy bedside and the boots and socks strewn around the room.

'Get in the shower. We've got work. Bring your weapon. I'll be outside.'

The man left, and Lee went to the kitchen and drank a jug of tap water. Stood under a blasting cold shower, his skin prickling where he'd been scratching on his face, neck, arms and chest. It was like he was still dreaming. Like he was a ghost instead of flesh and blood.

He dressed in jeans and a shirt. Put on his boots. There was a slowness to his movements that suggested soreness from the previous day's work-out in the gym, but he was still distant from himself, observing the weight of his legs and the tightness in his wrists and shoulders without the problem of pain, inflammation or stiffness. He transferred his cash to his pockets, and tucked the Luger into his jeans, then took it out and checked the safety.

He was alone in the house. Just the sound of distant traffic on Beaufort Street and the lofted singing of honeyeaters in the backyard.

The man was outside. He wore aviator sunglasses and a peaked cap, blue overalls and boots. He was a six-footer with lean, muscled arms and a face so sunburned that the skin on his cheeks had the look of old chamois. He stood beside a peach-coloured Commodore. Lee stopped short of him and put his hands on his hips. He wasn't going anywhere until he saw some proof.

'Get in.'

Lee got in his seat but didn't buckle up. The man gunned the engine and started to reverse.

'Wait!' Lee said, reaching for the handbrake.

The man stopped the car, nodded toward the glove box, waited for Lee to open the manila envelope. Inside was a mugshot of his father, wearing the brown leather jacket that Lee had bought him for his thirty-eighth birthday, those three months ago. The same goatee beard he'd worn the past year. The same chunky Bedouin silver ring on his right index finger, the heavy silver earrings. Same dark eyes, one noticeably smaller than the other. The scar that bisected his left eyebrow.

The mugshot board with its magnetic white letters was dated July twelve – two months ago – coinciding with his disappearance. The quality of the image was poor – a mugshot photocopied and put through a fax machine, but it was him alright. And that jacket made the date real.

His father looked out at the camera with an expression that Lee recognised. It was the look he gave when he was orating. Fierce but with his eyes scanning, hypervigilant. His confidence forced. In the photograph he appeared smaller, somehow diminished. He wouldn't be frightened, but he would be suffering. His intake of speed had been relentless over the past ten years and he drank whisky like water to level himself out. That supply would have been cut off the day he was locked up.

Lee's head was full of questions. Why hadn't his father contacted him, found a way to get a message out? Knowing that in the vacuum caused by his disappearance Lee would get in trouble with the others. Where was he being held?

As though reading his mind, the other man spoke. 'I don't know where he's locked up. I just know what you heard the other night. He's been charged with possession of dope and an unlicensed firearm, and he's in protective custody. And if you want to see him again, you got to pay your dues, for him, and for the cause.'

Lee put the picture back in its envelope, but the man took it and slung it onto his side of the dash. 'You don't get to keep that.'

They reversed onto the quiet street. Frankie had told him that it was a lower middle-class neighbourhood. Teachers. Public servants. Business owners. Geologists, engineers and the occasional tradie who'd done well on the mines. None of them aware, or caring, of what went on in house number thirty-three. It was an address, according to Frankie, that would be celebrated, come the revolution. That Lee Southern's name would be part of it, too.

Anybody else said that, Lee'd laugh in their face, but his eyes had been closed, his head cradled in her lap, Frankie's fingers stroking his scalp.

It was easier to ignore Frankie's comment and lie in her lap and listen to her reading Nietzsche from his thumbed copy of *Thus Spake Zarathustra*. He'd read it cover to cover all his life, and rarely understood its meaning, but Frankie recited it beautifully, like poetry. God might be dead, she said, but here were psalms for a godless world. 'I am a forest, and a night of dark trees: but he who is not afraid of my darkness, will find banks full of roses under my cypresses.' Lee didn't tell Frankie that he identified with Nietzsche mostly because of what finally broke him – the sight of a man beating a horse in the street. All of the words he'd written and his hopes for an evolved human consciousness brought down by the stubborn reality of human nature.

'You call me Brad. It isn't my real name, but it'll do.'

They were headed west, taking side streets until they crossed the train lines and freeway. Past a large football stadium, some light industry, then back into the suburbs, following the eastern edge of the train line as it turned south, past a cemetery where men and women in black jackets and dresses milled about in the carpark smoking and looking at their feet. Past a hospital, and then onto a small busy street, the footpath crowded with lunchtime traffic. The shoppers weren't much older than Lee, and he figured that they were near a university. Brad pulled the Commodore to the kerb outside a dentist's office clad in pink stucco. Turned off the ignition. Pocketed the manila envelope. Took off his sunglasses and turned to face Lee.

The engine ticked and cooled. Students wandered past.

'You got your weapon?'

Lee nodded.

'Loaded?'

'Yes.'

'Give it to me.'

'I don't think so.'

Brad shook his head. 'Then put it on the floor, where I can see it. Reach into the glove box and take out the paper bag.'

Lee did as he was asked. Inside the paper bag was another weapon, a black pistol – what would've once been called a lady's gun. As soon as he felt its weight he knew that it was wrong.

'This ain't even real. It's a toy gun.'

'No kidding. I'm in charge of you today. You're not taking a real gun on a job until I know what I'm dealing with.'

Lee saw it now – the R&I bank branch across the road, beside a bottle shop. He put the toy gun back in the bag.

'It's lunch hour. There's one staff member on duty. No cameras. You go in wearing your glasses and my cap, and show the teller this note, but you don't pass it over.'

The note read: *This is a robbery. Empty your till. No fuss and you won't get hurt.*

'You know the deal, kid. You want help getting to your

father, you help with our fighting fund.'

Brad put the cap on Lee's head. It was still warm. He folded the note and held it up. Lee looked at it, and at the bank.

He took up the paper bag, and twisted its mouth. He kept the note in his fingers.

'You've got five minutes. You're not out in five, I put my foot to the floor. This is a stolen vehicle and the plates are stolen. You don't know who I am, and even if you did, you even think of speaking, we got ways to shut you up. You're in the big league now. We got eyes and ears and supporters everywhere. Go and do what needs to be done.'

Lee's heart began to beat faster. His palms were clammy. His guts were a mess of nerves.

Brad put a hand on Lee's shoulder, shook him a little. 'Kid, have fun. This is the fun part of the job. Do this right, and everything's gonna be sweet for you, and your dad.'

Lee opened the car door and stepped into the sunlight. He wasn't dressed any different to the students who passed him in groups of two and three, hefting schoolbags, shopping bags, half-cartons and pizza boxes, and it was only the smiles on their faces and their self-conscious laughter that made him alien among them. He slipped in behind a boy with the arse hanging out of his jeans and a girl in tracksuit pants who were swaying into each other and holding hands. Lee turned across the road and kept his head down, and went to the door of the R&I. He forced himself to not look around the street.

Inside, it was just as Brad said, a small branch office with wood-veneer walls and one teller behind the bench – a young woman wearing a sleeveless uniform over a white collared shirt. She didn't look until he was right in front of her. Now he understood why a note was necessary, and he was grateful to the man in the car – he didn't trust himself to speak with any authority. She looked up and smiled and her eyes were pretty and her black eyeliner made her eyes even bluer and he passed her the note.

The toy gun remained in the paper bag while he watched her read. The odd thing was that her expression didn't change. She didn't appear frightened. Her eyes scanned his face like she was reading him and then she held out her hand. 'You got a bag or somethin?'

He only had the small paper bag, and felt a fool, and now he would have to speak, but she smirked and reached beneath her booth and took up a cotton money bag stamped with the R&I logo and she opened her till and started stuffing the bag with notes.

Lee watched her fingers skim the plastic scoops, flipping banded cash into the bag. Without being asked she went to the register next to her and opened its money tray and did the same. Lee kept an ear trained on the door and his eyes on the girl. When she was finished she passed him the stuffed bag with all the formality of someone serving a sandwich.

Lee tipped his cap and took the bag, making for the door. He heard her dial on a phone. Outside, the light was glaring, and Lee looked for the Commodore, which was turning across the street and cruising up to the footpath. All Lee had to do was climb inside. He buckled up and the Commodore moved round the corner into a suburban street that took them to the edge of Kings Park. Lee hadn't touched the money, and he stowed it beneath his seat along with the toy gun and the Luger and the cap. The Commodore rose along the bluff over the river that was calm as a pond, then drove through the woodland at precisely the speed limit until they reached the botanical gardens and pulled into a newly bitumenised carpark.

Now Brad turned in his seat, grinning.

'That girl,' Lee said. 'She was in on it, right?'

'Like I said, I'm not gonna take you on a job till I know what I'm dealing with. Pass me the bag.'

Lee reached under the seat and handed it over. Brad put his fingers into the bag and peered into it like a kid hungry for lollies. Lee looked at his own hands and watched the trembling dissipate as adrenalin dumped from his system. Brad passed him a lit cigarette and he took a satisfying drag and looked out the window at a king jarrah tree and the raked gravel beneath it. He wondered why Brad wasn't driving away instead of sitting in the empty carpark, something that would be noticeable to any copper on patrol, until he understood that this too was part of the test.

'You ever deploy?' Lee asked.

Brad chuckled. 'Nah, I lucked out. Joined up a few years after that commie prick Whitlam ended Vietnam. There was no war while I served, so like a proper white man, in seventy-eight I quit, and went lookin for one. Found what I was searching for in southern Africa. First Rhodesia, and then a few years later

I joined the SADF, and fought the nigger commies in Angola. The best years of my life, no doubt about it.'

Brad seemed just as amped by the robbery as Lee, or perhaps it was the memory of Africa. Aware that he was still being tested, Lee asked the kind of question his father might ask. 'What'd you make of apartheid as a system? They reckon it's not gonna last.'

Brad grimaced, shook his head. 'You think cos I fought there I cared about it? I did, I suppose. It was where I learned to be a white patriot. But I'm no South African. Apartheid is what you do when it's too late to do anything else.'

Brad's eyes had taken on an inflamed look, staring into the gardens but seeing something else. 'But it's not too late for us, and I'm proud to serve alongside you in the cause. You did good today. That's near ten thousand dollars. You got brass ones, I'll give you that.'

Brad patted him on the neck, climbed out of the Commodore and went to the phone booth at the edge of the carpark. Lee watched him drop a coin and dial, leaning into the shade of a gnarled old bloodwood, a hand shielding his mouth.

The keys were still in the ignition. The money was at his feet. All Lee had to do was shift over and ...

But Brad was looking at him. Nodding to the voice on the other end of the line. Hanging up and clenching his jaw and fists, striding back to the car.

'I've commended you and received authorisation to commend you officially. I was going to suggest the pub, but –'

'You got some bad news.'

Brad rolled the Commodore out onto the quiet park roads, the avenues of honour where the plaques of dead soldiers sat at the foot of each eucalyptus, thousands of them in every direction. There were Southerns numbered among the plaques, and on the walls of the memorial that they passed in silence, turning down the hill toward the city centre.

'Not bad news. Just … news.'

Brad parked the Commodore in front of a deli. He emerged a minute later with a copy of the *Daily News* that he dropped in Lee's lap. He didn't wait for Lee to begin reading, just started the car and pulled away.

There it was in black and white. The headline read DRUG LORD CHARGED WITH MURDER OF HIS BROTHER.

'This is how it starts. They turn us against one another.'

Lee didn't understand what Brad meant until he read deeper into the article. The arrest of Greg Downs for the murder of Brady Downs was made on the sworn testimony of a 'supergrass' who was in protective custody. The informer was not only a fellow gang member, but one of the Knights' leadership group, in retaliation for threats made against him, and his family.

Lee's father.

Not named, but it couldn't be anybody else.

Lee understood what that meant. For his father, and for him too.

Greg Downs, who'd taken over the leadership of the Knights when Lee's father disappeared, now charged with his brother's murder, on Lee's father's word.

'This can't be true.'

Brad stared down the road. 'Because he's no dog? He might be. Any father might be, if his family's threatened. And you're his only family.'

Lee dwelled on that for a minute, but it didn't smell right.

'You knew this already. What else?'

Brad pursed his lips, nodded. 'Only that he's been promised full immunity from prosecution, should he testify in court. And that he's safe. Somewhere Downs can't get at him.'

'There's nowhere that safe. Not for the money Downs'll be offering. Not if my father is the only witness ...'

Lee nearly said it. More rumours he'd heard over the years, of people who'd crossed the Knights, and got disappeared, or were found murdered in their cells. Drowned in their bathtubs.

But you don't say such things, to anyone.

Especially not an outsider.

'You think your father killed Brady Downs, like they say?'

'Let me out, here.'

They were in heavy traffic on Vincent Street. Brad glanced at the Luger in Lee's hand, pointed at his side.

'Put that away, son. I didn't mean anything by it. It was a dumb question to ask.'

'I won't tell you again.'

'You kill as many people as I have, Lee, you get to not caring whether you live or die. You can pull that trigger, or not pull that trigger, it's all the same to me.'

'Likewise.'

Brad glanced at him and saw that he wasn't joking. He pulled into the left lane. 'I'm gonna pretend this never happened. Let you think about what you've done. We're buildin something here. You won't find it easy to run from us. We're not some bunch of Geraldton dropkicks.'

The cars in front were slowing for the lights. Lee cracked the door, got ready.

'Son, we're the only ones who can help you. It's Friday. I need a hand changing the clutch on my Charger tomorrow afternoon. I'll swing by and pick you up round three. I'll have more news for you then. Something from your father. You'll see.'

They both looked at the bag of cash on the floorpan. Brad shook his head. The car pulled to a stop and Lee climbed out, tucked the Luger into his jeans and started walking north. He walked past schools breaking for the day, and offices where men and women stared at computer screens. Pubs where men in overalls clutched at their drinks. Factories where the hiss and grind of machinery made a kind of music. He walked across the park where the blacks were gathered by the lake, cackling and shouting at one another. He walked with his shoulders hunched and his head down. People on the footpath saw him coming and stepped out of his way.

He left Beaufort Street and took suburban roads up the long hill toward the house where he hoped Frankie was waiting for him. He hadn't examined why she might be waiting for him, or why she was caring for him, because he didn't care.

He felt sick by the time he reached the street. His skin was clammy and his eyes were watering. He felt hot and cold.

The front door was locked and he shouldered at it, once, twice, until he heard footsteps in the darkened hall. Frankie took one look at him and waved him in. He went straight into her room and sat on the bed.

The hours felt like minutes. He wasn't aware of his fingernails on his skin, only the sensation of pinpricks rising to the surface of his flesh and a pleasure that flared when he scratched. Inside his head there was a blossoming of light that surged through his body. He was aware of noises and the pressing of cold air on his eyelids and the gravity that pinned him to the bed, and everything was better as long as he was still, and quiet, and kept his eyes closed.

But there was a new weight on the bed and then a hand on his face, caressing him. 'Wake up, Lee.'

'I am awake.'

'I know. I could tell from your breathing.'

He opened his eyes and it was night. Frankie scratched his head, smiling down at him, backlit by the glow from the hall. 'Get dressed. We're going out.'

11.

Lee couldn't help himself – he liked the music. Loud and ferocious in the low dark room, all hard-charging guitar and manic drums with a solid melody weaving through bouts of chaos; the strutting and clowning of the lead man. There were a few dozen people dancing, nearly all of them males, slamming into each other and leaping about the place. The odd fist thrown. Some girls bobbing on the edges. The stage was low and vibrating with the stomping and smashing drums. It was so loud that Lee's ears felt like they were being torn. He didn't get to see a lot of live music back home and he'd never seen anything like this crowd. Some of them were in their late twenties, like the band, but lots of them were his age, skinheads and the odd punk, and they'd all taken a deal of care with their clothes and hair. Some were English, but most were local kids.

The club was called Minsky's and according to Frankie this was the first time it'd hosted what she called her people. Her hair was teased out and her eyeliner was heavy. She wore a tartan skirt and boots. A singlet and no bra. A faux knuckleduster ring on her left hand. She seemed to know everyone in the room, although most of the time it was too loud to talk. She sat on a pink vinyl pouf next to Lee, beside a couch made of the same material. People passed by and she nodded and waved, squeezed Lee's hand.

The taxi had dropped them an hour earlier, and Lee immediately recognised the street. It was the same one from earlier today. The bank there on the corner, dark now. Students on the footpaths, carrying bags and pizza boxes.

Every now and then some student-looking punters rose up the entrance stairs, although they didn't get very far. A couple of them took a look and turned on their heels. One drunk young man in jeans and flannel walked into the crowd and was set upon by skinhead boys crustying him on the top of the head, and when he started swinging, they took turns kicking him in the arse until he was down and crawling back to the stairs.

The band now paused their set and the singer leapt into the crowd, was backslapped and offered a jug.

'That's Nigel,' Frankie shouted, pointing out the bass player. 'He just got back from a few months playing with Skrewdriver in England.'

The bass player saw her pointing and walked through the crowd and leaned down and kissed her on the forehead. He wore a cardigan over a swastika t-shirt. Jeans and plain black shoes. He took a cigarette from Lee's pack and Frankie lit it for him. He drifted off toward the crowded bar.

'They're really called Final Solution?' Lee asked.

Frankie grinned. 'I *know*.'

Lee wondered if she'd taken something else, because her eyes were dilated and she talked in blurts and wouldn't sit still. They were drinking lukewarm beer. She wouldn't let him drink anything else because of how high he was.

It was true. He was awake because of the noise and the sense of violence in the room, but he still felt like he was floating on a carpet, the surges of pleasure weakened now to flushes of warmth.

With no music, the dancers started looking for distraction, shoving one another. More punches were thrown. One boy who was punched in the mouth wiped away the blood and forced a bloody kiss on his attacker, rolling around on the floor.

An older skinhead came to them. He nodded to Frankie but leaned down to Lee.

'I'll fight you for her,' he said quietly in a northern English accent.

Frankie heard too. 'Go away, Geordie.'

'Follow me out to the carpark and we'll fight for her. How you gonna protect her from scum like me if you're too chicken to fight for her? That what happened to your face already? You wanna defend your woman, right?'

'Fuck off, Geordie,' said Frankie.

Lee looked him over. The guy was heavy-set and wore the uniform of stovepipe jeans and boots. 'Love' and 'Hate' on his knuckles. A walking cliché, but Lee had the feeling that he'd been there from the beginning.

Lee was just about to get up and take him on, but Frankie put her hand on his thigh, squeezed forcefully. 'Don't worry about Geords. He's just fucking around.'

Lee looked up into his face, which cracked with a cold smile. 'Yeah, I'm just fucken around with ya, mate. Hang on. He doesn't *know*, does he? Your prince charming?'

'Know what?' Lee asked.

The big man roared, scratched his head, walked away.

'Ah, nothing,' Frankie answered. 'This is about to get ugly.'

'It sure is.'

The punters stranded on the dance floor were capering about and calling for the band to return, but the lead singer gave them the finger from the bar. One or two started kicking at the base of the stage. Another few started pulling the soundproof cladding from the walls. Beer glasses rained onto the stage, smashing over the rear wall.

'Just in time.'

Lee hadn't seen the young woman enter until she leaned over Frankie, and they began kissing. It was a long, passionate kiss.

Geordie shouted from the bar, 'Give a man a go would ya, ya dirty lezzos!'

Frankie's finger went up, but she was smiling in the kiss. Geordie too was smiling, hefting a table over his head and launching it onto the dance floor.

The young woman kissing Frankie broke off first, turned to him. Frankie laughed. 'Believe you two have met.'

He almost didn't recognise her, with her purple eyeliner and lipstick, the baggy jumper and gelled-up hair. It was the girl from the bank.

She took Lee's hand and reached over and took Frankie's arm. 'I'm Jen. Let's get out of here before the cops arrive. I've had enough of the cops today, thanks to you two.'

She nudged Lee in the ribs and then they were headed for the door. Outside, there was fighting in the street and someone had thrown a bin through a shop window. They walked to the corner of the highway and flagged a taxi. The two women were laughing about Lee in the bank. Frankie tickled his chin while he walked, her arm around Jen.

'So *serious*, were you? I bet!'

It wasn't Frankie having a girlfriend that surprised Lee. Frankie and Lee had spent many nights together in her bed, but they'd never made love – the gear they shared was enough. Lee was more surprised by what Jen had said. '… thanks to you *two*.' Not that he should've been surprised. He'd been housed with Frankie for a reason, and while he didn't know where she fit in, he didn't particularly care, because his blood was still buzzing with warmth and they were headed back for more.

PART II

12.

School was nearly out. Lee sat in the truck and checked his reflection in the rear-view mirror. The bruising on his face was gone. There was a pale scar on the bridge of his nose and a strip of sandpapery skin on his left cheekbone, but other than that he looked no different from when he'd last seen Emma those eleven months ago.

Despite the letter she'd written, he wondered whether she'd forgiven him, would want to see him again. He didn't plan to tell her about his current situation but he craved the sound of her voice and that playful sparkle in her eyes, the feeling of her soft skin against his own, however brief that might be.

He'd robbed four banks now and was getting to like it. He wore a kerchief over his face like an old-time bushranger and Brad wore the same. The banks they were knocking over were two-man operations, and there was always the driver in the car outside. His name was Mick and he was also a veteran, now a prison guard on the night shift. It was all done with military precision, from the planning to the execution.

Nobody got hurt, although Brad put the fear into the staff and customers to the extent that they didn't remember too clearly. The identikit pictures published in the papers were way off.

Lee checked his driver's wing mirror to see if there were any students leaking out of the school grounds, but all was silent. He'd scouted Emma's exit from the school. She always left by the main entrance with the same group of friends, walking the two hundred metres to the nearest bus stop. She looked happy as she undid her braids and shook out her hair, something that none of the other girls did.

He wondered if she'd seen the identikit pictures in the daily papers, and thought of him, even though the resemblance was poor. He was described as young and of medium build. Average everything. Brown hair and eyes beneath the grey cap.

The truth was that his new life had become normal, from the bank jobs to working his tow truck solo, the other drivers of True West Towing leaving him alone. He only went to the depot to fill up his Ford, or to deposit those vehicles that were written off. He'd towed a Mitsubishi people-mover with a busted transmission on his way to Emma's school, had dropped it off at the mechanics workshop in Spearwood run by Gerry, the boxer. After that he went to Gerry and Frank's boxing gym to train for an hour. He showered there, so he'd be cleaned up. He trained there most days of the week now, letting himself in with the key Gerry had given him. They were alright, those two.

A single girl in the full uniform walked out of the front

building, holding her straw hat against the sea breeze and wincing into the sun. Lee rolled down the sleeves of his check shirt and popped the buttons closed. He was fixing himself now. Frankie had shown him how to avoid infection, and although the ground-up morphine tablets she sourced from the hospital were pure and clean, he knew that the small red spots in the crux of his arm and on the back of his wrist were there, and that was enough to want to hide them. He didn't get much of a high anymore, but he still looked forward to the end of every day, when he got home and fixed himself. During the day he cracked the pills with his teeth and swallowed the bitter juices. The pills kept him on the level, where he needed to be.

He saw her then. Not dressed in the long woollen skirt and blazer, but in a dark blue tracksuit with white tennis shoes. Lee climbed out. He walked to the front of the truck and took his position. He was more nervous than before the last bank robbery. He straightened his collar and shot his cuffs and leaned on the roo bar, trying not to look too obvious. Such a country boy, he thought, with his check shirt, jeans and workboots. He remembered his sunglasses and took them off, waved a hand over his shorn head.

She was with the same group of girls as every day, taller than the rest of them. She shook out her long black hair, something she'd inherited from her Chinese-Burmese mother. Her lips were a natural red and her cheeks were rosy.

He wasn't going to say anything. She would see him, and her reaction would tell him what he needed to know.

She hefted her bag that contained a hockey stick strapped to its side, which kept slipping. She fell behind her friends, who hadn't noticed.

They passed and looked him up and down, not liking what they saw. The hick. The dirty old truck.

She was in the process of catching them up when she saw him. Her face broke into a smile. Her eyes, so warm and brown.

'That stick for use on me?' he asked.

'Might be if you don't come and give me a hug.'

He stepped to her and she slipped into his arms. Her hair smelled the same, like pine needles. It was as though the last eleven months weren't real.

One of her friends, a short pale girl who under her boater hat looked like a cartoon duck, was right there. 'Em, everything ok?'

Emma didn't introduce him, or speak. He felt her nod on his shoulder, and the girl stepped away. Emma leaned back and framed his face with her hands, stood on her toes and planted a kiss on his mouth.

*

They sat at a café table on Fremantle's main street. Most of the other people were old men and none of them were speaking English. There were some heavy-looking boys with ratty mullets dressed in black jeans standing around a red Monaro on the street. One or two of them glared at him, and he looked away.

They hadn't talked about it on the drive down, and he could

see that she didn't want to talk about it now. Perhaps later, once things were settled.

He'd lied to her and said that he was working on a farm near Albany, was just up for a few days to buy parts for his truck. But he'd never been that far south, and hoped she didn't ask questions.

He thought about telling her that he was working on the tuna-boats, but that would be a big mistake. It was a prawn trawler that her favourite cousin, David, was found hanged on, there in Geraldton Harbour. A middle-class city boy who'd made the mistake of telling Danny Hislop, by then a Knights prospect like Lee, to fuck off. They were all drinking, and Lee and Emma had been kissing on the bow, their legs hanging over the polished steel surface of the night water.

They shouldn't have brought David along. He was funny and anxious and didn't fit in, didn't know what the rules were. Danny was ribbing him a bit but Lee knew that he was holding back, too. But it obviously didn't feel like that to David. Both Lee and Emma heard the 'fuck off', as did everyone else on the boat, and down the jetty. Then a nervous giggle. Lee stood over them where they were seated on the deck, sharing a bottle of green ginger wine, and a joint. Danny looked up and met his eyes, and Lee looked for it, that meanness he was famous for, aroused. But Lee didn't see it, and that was his biggest mistake.

No matter how many times Emma pleaded with David to join them, to come back home with them, he refused, insisting that he and Danny were going to finish the bottle and go to a nightclub. He was happy-stoned. His face flushed with the wine.

They left him and returned to the Sandman, made love at the base of the dunes on the back beach, the doors open to the starry sky and the sound of surf on the reefs. Then Lee dropped Emma home.

David was found the next morning, hanging from the steel boom of the net-winch, there in the harbour. There was no note. No sign of a struggle.

No arrest made. They were all questioned and everyone told the same story. That David and Danny were the last ones on the boat. Danny claiming that David was too drunk to walk, had wanted to sleep on the boat. So he'd left him, like the others left him, and drove home to his parents' servo. Danny's father confirming his time of arrival.

Only Emma and Lee mentioned the 'fuck off'. Both of them admitting that Danny didn't appear too concerned. Both of them knowing what had happened, but not able to prove it.

Emma's family drove down to Perth for the funeral, and Emma never came back. Her father quit his principal's position. He refused to speak to Lee about it. He wouldn't give him a number to call.

Lee sought out Danny Hislop. There were no witnesses at the plantation fifty K east of the town, on a track that only a few Knights knew about. Lee had long suspected that the bush weed Danny was selling in ounce bags to the fishermen he worked alongside was harvested from a Knights' crop.

Lee caught him on a bend that threaded two granite rocks.

He'd parked and blocked the track, knew the sound of Danny's old HQ utility. He smoked and waited and thought about what he was planning to do. The places it might take him. What it might mean for his father, now that Danny was a prospect too. Both their fathers leaders in the hierarchy. Danny's father a volatile man. Said to be a contract killer for the bikies. Like everything else to do with the Knights, it might be true, or it might be bullshit, although most people in town played it safe and assumed it was true, laughed at his jokes and steered clear. Danny was also a nephew of the Downs brothers, also in the hierarchy. Together, the three of them could make things very difficult for Lee's father.

The sun was drifting to the mallee scrub horizon of gnarled shapes and fire-blackened skin. The flies were bad and gathered on the sweat patches over Lee's shoulders and back. He waved them away and they arose in a swarm and then returned. They crept into his eyes and mouth, seeking moisture.

There was a loaded .303 rifle standing behind a termite mound to his left. There was a shillelagh leant against a wizened acacia next to the track. He had a knife strapped to his belt.

Just in case.

He took off his flannel shirt, sunglasses and hat. He didn't want anything interfering with his movements or his vision.

He heard the ute sloughing over the sandy track, whirring through the gears, then the faint sounds of AC/DC's 'Hells Bells', incongruous out there in the great openness. The sky arched wide and blue above him, emptying his head of everything except what he needed to do.

The ute nosed around the nearest boulder, Danny's eyes widening as he realised that he was hemmed in by rock. He stopped the car and put it into reverse, but the boggy track and the angle of the turn gave Lee time to reach the door. Danny locked it and began to wind the window up but he was too late. Lee punched Danny so many times that he lost count. Got his body half in the cab and started slamming Danny's head on the steering wheel, the horn blaring with every blow, Danny losing consciousness. Lee unlocked the door and dragged him onto the track.

Now he went to work on Danny with his boots, curled into the foetal position or trying to get to his knees, wheezing blood from his broken mouth. Lee remembered his father's words. How back in the old days Danny was the kind of boy that the village elders would get rid of, make it look like a hunting accident or a fall from a height. Lee hadn't planned on murder but it was like his father's words were guiding him. He knew with perfect clarity what his father would do. Kill Danny and bury his body deep. Drop his car in town.

Nobody would ever know except Lee, a secret that he'd nurse for the rest of his life. Plenty of men around town had the same secret. You could see it in their faces. Not the secret, but the guarding of a secret.

There was sand stuck to the blood on Danny's face, in his eyes. His mouth bubbling blood. Lee looked down upon his work. Broken ribs. Broken jaw. A shattered wrist.

It would be kinder to kill him.

Danny wasn't complaining any longer, as though he wanted it to end, as though he was complicit.

Lee had the shillelagh, tossing it from hand to hand, looking down at the fragile egg.

He raised it and stepped.

Made to swing down.

Feinted, and tried again.

But his arm wouldn't fall.

He spat and tried again, failed to strike, again.

There were tears in his eyes. They stung, made it hard to see.

He stepped back.

It wasn't him.

Wasn't in him.

The drive into town took an hour, but he wasn't aware, didn't remember it except for the times he stopped to dry-heave on the graded shoulder.

Later, the shame settled in.

At what he had done, and what he had failed to do.

There would be consequences, for both.

*

She was looking at him, the coffee mug at her lips. 'Did you have to leave because of Danny Hislop?'

Lee nodded. She'd obviously been thinking about it. Smart of her not to ask what he'd done.

'Can you go back?'

'No.'

'I'm sorry about your father.'

Lee looked at her then, wondered what she knew. Did she mean that his father was missing, or that he'd turned dog?

He changed the subject, asked her about the new school. It was alright, she said. She wasn't used to the uniform or the rules dictating ladylike behaviour, and sometimes she felt like pulling her hair out. But her aunt Josephine still blamed her father for David's death, which had occurred while her son was under his care. Her father had become withdrawn and depressed. Emma was trying to do the right thing.

There was so much that Lee wanted to tell her. That he needed to tell someone. But she would be disgusted to hear that he was working with people like Kinslow and his boys, even if he didn't have a choice. Lee's friends had known better than to make comment when he started dating Emma, but she'd picked up on their disapproval anyway, and they'd talked about it – Emma describing how much crap her mother had to put up with, both in Geraldton but also back in Perth. Lee already aware how much Emma was mocked at school, until she got with Lee, and then at least the comments about her Asian features were no longer made to her face.

He enjoyed sitting with her in the warm afternoon sunshine, the sounds of life around them. Her hair blowing in the faint breeze. The sparkle of light in her eyes, squinting a little. He thought about walking over to the docks. Or buying her something in the streets of shops that surrounded them.

She needed to be home by six.

He looked down the road. Saw the sign, just past an old two-storey gold-rush building with a balcony over the street.

'Hey, you ever been ice skating?' he asked.

She smiled. 'No, never. You?'

13.

It was dark when Lee got back to Frankie's house. She was waiting in her room. 'I was worried you wouldn't be home in time. Take a seat. You've only got ten minutes.'

Lee warmed to her smile. 'Why? What's up?'

'A reward. For your contributions.'

'Very mysterious.'

Frankie passed him the gram packet she'd already opened. He tapped out a mound of powder and began the routine while Frankie applied eyeliner in front of a hand mirror.

'We going out?'

'We are, but not to the same place, not together, I mean. I'm going to a gig at the Shents.'

'And me?'

'That's confidential.'

There was no use pressing her. They'd spent a lot of time together, but Lee was no closer to understanding where she fit in with Kinslow and the old man's organisation, or even what she believed. Ever since that first day, she hadn't returned to the differences between them, except to say that she judged people by their actions, not their words. She'd taken on the role of the proud big sister. She always seemed to know what he'd done, and where and when.

Lee found the vein in the back of his wrist and capped his fit, put it on the bedside table. He wiped his eyes and rolled his neck. He closed his eyes and felt the surge in his blood. When he opened his eyes Brad was standing in the lintel of the open doorway, sneering down at him. He wasn't dressed for a job but was wearing workboots, ironed King Gee khakis and a tight Bonds tee. Brad ignored Frankie like he always did, angling his head toward the road.

*

They drove down the Kwinana Freeway until they reached the turn-off for Jandakot Airport, then turned east toward the hills. Soon the new housing developments disappeared and then it was bush blocks and then just bush. Lee knew better than to ask where they were headed, although the further they drove, the more wary he became. He was unarmed – the Luger was back in the locked compartment of his truck. Brad had frisked him and emptied his pockets before they'd left, allowing him only his money and driver's licence.

Brad was silent until they reached the floodlit walls of a fenced perimeter. Inside the fence was a higher concrete wall with watchtowers and razor wire. The sheet-metal sign said 'Canning Vale Prison', its lower half stained red with bore water rust that in the darkness looked like blood. The carpark was empty and the buildings outside the wall were dark.

Brad killed the engine and turned in his seat. 'You know what this means. This is a once-only thing. We had to call in favours. You look the wrong way or say the wrong word and I'll pull you out and deal with you. The rules are simple. You don't mention any operational activities. You don't mention the beating you took. You don't mention us by name. You don't say where you're living or any of that shit. You've got five minutes. I'll be listening in, to enforce the rules.'

Brad looked at his watch, which had gone five past eight. 'Fuck.'

The front gate was lit by high-pressure sodium lamps mounted above CCTV cameras, although the doorway was hidden in shadow. Brad took something from his back pocket that he clearly didn't want to show. It was a snap-hinged and laminated ID card that, together with his open wallet and Lee's driver's licence, was raised to the security camera mounted inside the doorway. The front door clicked open, followed by a loud buzz that echoed in the next chamber. Brad repeated the process, Lee trying to steal a glance at the badge inside his wallet before he returned it to his pocket.

Without looking at him, Brad grunted, 'Good try. What'd I tell you about looking wrong?'

Four prison guards at a low brushed-steel desk ignored them as they passed, continuing to read the paper, pen crosswords and scan CCTV screens. They were met at the end of the hall by a TRG officer in his regulation dark blue coveralls and boots. There was no rank insignia or name tag on his uniform and he didn't look familiar. He nodded at Brad, then looked at Lee.

'I checked him already. We're good to go.'

The TRG officer turned and they followed him down a corridor. Inside a room to their left, a dozen more TRG men worked out on weight machines or watched television, their chest armour, helmets, batons and shotguns within easy reach.

'Keep yer eyes to yerself,' Brad hissed.

They were waved through two more gates by disinterested guards before they entered the darkened visiting room. Brad flicked a switch and ceiling fluorescents in steel cages buzzed and filled the space with a sickly light. The wooden desks looked like they'd been rescued from a high school, scratched with graffiti and images of dragons, knives and breasts. The chairs were no different, and Brad kicked one toward Lee, nodded for him to sit. Brad and the TRG officer went and stood at opposite walls.

Now it was real. Lee'd done everything asked of him to make this possible, but that was only one side of the equation. His father was proud and wouldn't take to being stood over, or blackmailed. Brad's demeanour in the car was hard to read. For a while there, Lee'd thought he was being taken out into the bush to be deep-sixed. Presumably his father, then, had also been playing their game, doing what was asked of him to keep Lee safe. His father had what they wanted, but this meeting was something else, too – a demonstration of their power.

Behind the steel door he could hear the buzz-echoes of other doors opening and slamming shut. The nerves in his stomach rose into his chest. He felt blood in his face as his heart beat faster. His father would see the smack in his eyes.

The nerves helped. Lee gathered himself and sat forward. The door buzzed and clicked open. An old screw with a paunch and silver hair entered the room, swinging keys on a chain. He looked at the TRG officer and nodded, stepped away.

Jack Southern shuffled into the open doorway. He was cuffed. Even from a distance Lee saw the note in his fingers. His father took his time scanning their faces before stepping through. He wore the prison green tracksuit and plastic slip-ons. His eyes remained cool under their gaze until he was at the desk, playing a role. He'd done plenty of time after he got out of the army, before Lee was old enough to remember.

Finally, their eyes met.

'Fuck this.'

The words were Lee's. He stood, stepping around the desk, took his father in an embrace. He felt the note slide into his left hand. His father's gauntness was confirmed in the seconds it took Brad and the TRG officer to reach them, and break them apart. In his urgency to embrace his father Lee held on tight, had even lifted him momentarily from the floor, was shocked at how light he was. His fingers felt bone and sinew. Ribs, spine, shoulderblade.

'Sit the fuck down.'

The TRG officer pushed his father onto a chair. Lee hid the note and raised his hands in surrender. Brad and the TRG officer returned to their walls. The screw at the door twirled his keys, looking at the floor, scraping something off the sole of his left boot.

'Dad. I'm alright. I got the Ford from Uncle Gary. We fixed a towing rig onto it. I'm working it ...'

There wasn't much time. Lee gave the summary, leaving out the boxing gym and Emma.

'Show me yer arms.'

Lee knew what that meant. He opened his wrists.

'I suppose you reckon I'm a hypocrite, but –'

'I understand.'

'Plenty of time in here, to think. Nothing but fucken time. Nothin but fucken thinkin. We can talk about all ... this ... me, you, when I get out. But you're lookin good. Reckon you've even grown. You got a confidence about you. It suits.'

'You too,' Lee said. 'Bit paler, but then I guess you don't get much sun.'

'Thanks for lyin. I look like shit because I feel like shit –'

'What about the meditation? Your exercises?'

Jack Southern shrugged. 'Like I say, nothing but fucken thinkin.'

Lee bowed his head, lowered his voice. 'Why didn't you get a message to me? I thought you were dead.'

'I tried, son,' he whispered. 'But listen now. I've heard on the wire that it was Danny Hislop who killed his uncle. Danny killed Brady Downs because he refused to move against me. Greg Downs is refusing to believe it.'

Lee's stomach tumbled. He knew immediately what had happened. 'Because of what I did to Danny?'

Jack Southern blinked, a nod. 'I always told you what Danny was. He killed his uncle then framed me up. And it worked. I had to disappear and you're on the bolt.'

'What are you gonna do?' Lee asked.

'Not me. You.'

Brad clapped his hands. The noise was sharp in the locked room and it made his father flinch. Lee wondered if Brad had overheard their conversation. 'Dad, you eating? You got stuff to read?'

Brad kicked through the table, sent it clattering away. 'I said, that's *enough*. Family reunion's over. We done our part here.'

Brad stood between them. Lee's father put his cuffed hands out, a question. Brad nodded, and Lee shook his father's hands, looked into his eyes, didn't like what he saw. Shame there, and a diamond of light, the beginning of tears.

Then the screw took him by the shoulder and led him away. He didn't turn back while the door was opened. He was pushed through, and then the door was shut.

'Take the note out of your pocket. The one your father gave you.' Brad smirked, his hand out, but thought better of it. 'Read it aloud.'

Lee took out the tightly folded stick of paper. His father's spidery handwriting on a corner ripped from a red lined sheet. 'It says … *Right enough in here. Under the pump, as you'd expect. Never mind about me.*'

Lee passed it over. Brad read it again and poked Lee in the chest, leaned closer. 'But you're not going to RUN, are you,

Lee? Not if you want to see your father again.'

The TRG officer tapped his watch, went to the door. He pressed a buzzer, turned off the lights.

Lee was grateful for the darkness. Now he could wipe his eyes.

14.

Brad and his ex-army buddies had rigged up a winch to get the engine out of Brad's Charger. Lee stood and waited while they broke it down on a tarp on the front lawn. He was there because Brad wanted to talk to him about a development with his father. Lee was hoping for another note, or the promise of further visits, but when Lee asked, Brad muttered under his breath and reached for a socket. He and his mates were on the tail end of an all-nighter – Lee knew the signs. Bleary red eyes, shaking hands and talking through gritted teeth and clenched jaws.

Nollamara was mostly a public housing area and there were a lot of blacks and Vietnamese in the other houses on the street. They walked past and looked at the white men and their oil-stained hands sweating in the sun, until Brad or one of his friends noticed them and then they were rained with abuse. The tarp beside the Charger was piled with tyre irons, heavy spanners and lump hammers, and nobody said anything back. Brad had earlier told Lee that he refused to move to another suburb because he wanted to be reminded, every day, of what their world would one day look like. A few white men surrounded by darkies and chinks.

On his way to Nollamara, Lee had stopped at a Beaufort Street deli to buy a coffee and some smokes. Over the past week he'd noticed how quickly the anti-Asian posters on the bins, phone booths, electricity exchange boxes and vacant shopfronts had been torn away or painted over, but a new set of the same posters had been put up last night. Lee watched the reactions of the mainly elderly Asian men and women as they noticed the posters. Every one of them ducked their heads and looked away until they noticed the next sign, and then the next, their shoulders slumped and not meeting the eyes of those approaching. Lee wasn't the only person to watch their reactions. He saw one young man in a bus driver's uniform smirk and mutter something under his breath at a passing old lady, who looked to the ground and didn't respond. It wasn't hard to imagine how she felt – made unwelcome in her own country. If there had only been one poster Lee might have torn it down, but there were dozens on this block, and hundreds further along the street.

Lee finished his cigarette. Brad was elbow-deep in the engine block and feeling around for metal shavings. He looked up and told Lee to get him and the others a beer.

One thing that last night's prison meeting demonstrated was the reality of his father's vulnerability. Brad obviously had contacts in the TRG and among the guards. His father would likely be held in the Seg, the most secure facility there, a prison within the prison, but the Knights too had contacts in the custodial service. If they learned where Jack Southern was imprisoned, then they'd find a way to get at him.

Lee went inside to get the beers. He opened the fridge door and heard moaning from the laundry that led onto the backyard. In the laundry was a man bound to a chair, wearing the black hood. His feet had been burned. The familiar black carbon residue from a zippo lighter framed the red welts on the soles of his curled feet. The big toe on his right foot was bloody. The toenail was missing. Lee pulled off the hood. A young Chinese or Vietnamese man looked at him with unfocused eyes. His cheekbones were bruised and there was blood around his mouth.

'Please. Let me go. I won't tell police. I have money. I call my parents.'

Lee tossed the hood into the laundry sink. He returned to the fridge and got a sixpack of Emu Bitter, went back outside.

Brad was speaking, his voice spidery with fatigue, the speed wearing off. Lee needed to be careful. He put the beers on the tarp and stood back, waited for the rant to end. Brad's mates rolled their eyes – they didn't need to hear it again. 'I've travelled to all the shitholes of this world, and all of it's a shithole compared to what we got here. The people here think that their wealth means that they're strong, that it'll keep them safe, but they're not, and it won't. They think they want democracy, because it's the best system for the weak to lord it over the strong. But they'll give up democracy in an instant as long as they don't lose their cars, their houses and holidays. As long as it's someone else getting kicked, and not them. Deep down, your average man just wants a leader. Stability. To see the same face and know the job is being done. We can provide that certainty. And those who don't like it can fuck off. Mark my words. Within thirty years, whites will be a minority in this country. Asians are better workers and consumers, and that's all that any capitalist society asks of its people. Whites will be useful in the army, because that's our nature, but we won't have any real power. We got to –'

Lee let the words wash over him until Brad lost his train of thought.

'The man inside. I'm taking him to the hospital.'

Brad laughed. 'The fuck you are. That slopehead spoke back to me.'

Lee kept his voice even. 'Yeah, I know, but that was last night ...'

Lee let the words hang, looking around at the faces of Brad's friends. None of them spoke against him. Lee could imagine how it went down. Seemed like a good idea at the time. Brad all fired up and wanting to demonstrate how they used to interrogate kaffir prisoners in Africa. Brad's friends were ex-army, but too young to have seen war. They wouldn't have seen that kind of pain inflicted, heard those sounds.

Brad kept ratcheting a small bolt on a rocker cover.

'You know where he lives, right?' Lee said.

Brad laughed. 'Fucken oath we do. And that he's got two sisters. His father's got a barber shop in Northbridge.'

'So he's not gonna talk.'

Brad looked to his mates. Mick, the screw, nodded. They were supposed to be professionals, and Brad had put them at risk.

'Alright then, fucken take him. I'd forgotten he was there. Save me the trouble of wringing his gook neck, diggin a grave. But if he talks, it's on you. We'll all say that you were here. That you did the burnin, took off his toenail.'

Lee went back inside the house. He untied the man's feet and hands, but the man didn't get up. His eyes didn't believe. He cowered whenever Lee moved.

He was broken.

Lee held up the hood. 'I'm going to take you home. You don't talk, right? They weren't joking about your family. You seen already. These are bad men.'

The man nodded.

'Can you walk? Your feet …'

The man got up quickly, braced himself on the sink, putting weight onto the outsides of his feet. He didn't appear to be in any pain. He was still in shock.

'Put this on. They need to see that it's on.'

The man accepted the hood, slipped it onto his head, the heavy material settling on his shoulders.

Lee took the man's arm and draped it around his neck. They made slow time out into the backyard, the man crying inside the hood. Lee opened the back gate and they entered the garage where his truck was parked. Lee didn't know what he'd do if Brad changed his mind. He got the man up into the cab's passenger seat, went around to the driver's side, cranked the engine and reversed into the sunlight. Brad and his friends were sprawled in a circle, smoking and finishing their beers. None of them looked as Lee rolled into the street, changed gear and drove away.

'I'll take you to the hospital,' he said when they reached the first corner.

The man was still crying, gently now, his shoulders trembling. 'Please. No hospital. Take me to my parents. I don't want my wife, children, to see.'

Lee memorised the Balcatta address, which wasn't far.

'Why do you help me? Why are you friends with those men?'

'They're not my friends.'

'But you know them.'

Lee didn't answer. The pity he'd felt for the man and the disgust he felt toward Brad were building into a fierce anger. His fingers were clenched on the wheel, but he didn't trust himself to speak. Everything he thought of saying sounded like a justification.

'Why they do this to me?'

Lee patted the man's shoulder. This time, he didn't flinch. Lee pulled off the hood and slung it out the window. The man looked straight ahead. Lee didn't reply, but thought instead of Brad, and Robbie; Greg Downs and Danny Hislop. Men who enjoyed hurting people.

Lee didn't believe in evil. Their cruelty had nothing to do with a transcendent being, or even the poison of their beliefs.

'I'm sorry', he said quietly, and then, 'what's your name?'

15.

Lee stopped at the Osborne Park depot to fill his truck. He'd helped the Vietnamese man to his front doorstep, and rung the bell. Lee would be remembered, but didn't care. The man, whose name was Robert, had passed out in the truck, head nodding and sliding in his seat. He'd been tied to a chair overnight and tortured – sleeping not a priority when you think it's your last night on earth. Robert's parents lived in an old salmon-brick house with a red-painted driveway and planter boxes filled with herbs. A silky terrier yapped as Lee helped Robert down the path made of concrete pavers. The doorbell didn't work, and Lee rapped his knuckles on the security screen. The silky continued to yap and the house smelled of dog and herbs he couldn't name. He heard a door open and bare feet on the lino floor. An old woman looked at them both and the truck on the verge, narrowing her eyes until she saw that her son was hurt.

She'd yelped, put her hands to her mouth. An old man pushed past her and opened the door. Lee unlocked Robert's arm from around his neck and gave the arm to his father. The old man's eyes said that he'd seen some things in his lifetime. Nobody spoke, and Lee had backed away.

*

When the Ford's tank was full, Lee capped the mouth and replaced the nozzle. He kept his back to the depot office. He didn't feel like talking to anyone, didn't trust himself to hold his tongue.

He hadn't seen Kinslow much over the past weeks. There was an election coming up, and Kinslow and his boys were busy with their poster campaign. They were also distributing pamphlets in letterboxes that lately carried a picture of Kinslow standing beside one of his trucks. He was running as a candidate for the APM, the Australian Patriotic Movement. A smiling working-class white man and small-business owner, worried about jobs for the young, when so many Asian migrants were moving in and stealing them.

The True West guard dog, Bessie, a bulldog who'd been sleeping on her chain, stood and shivered and went over to the shed beside the depot office. Lee locked the bowser just as Kinslow emerged, smoking a cigarette. He waved Lee over, as inscrutable as always. If he was angry at Lee for helping himself to the depot fuel and keeping his tow earnings to himself, he kept his counsel.

Kinslow ground out his ciggie with the toe of his boot, nodded for Lee to follow him inside. The last time Lee entered the shed it'd been decked out with Nazi and Southern Cross flags, and a framed picture of Hitler. Shooting targets, with their Asiatic faces and bodies riddled with holes taken from some army gun range. Malcolm Fraser, the Liberal PM who'd let in all the Vietnamese boat people, was represented on the dartboard.

But now it was empty except for trestle tables laden with posters and pamphlets, maps of the local streets and a bubbling urn on milk crates in the corner.

Kinslow saw the look on Lee's face and nodded. 'Don't worry, we sweep it for bugs every day. We've found three so far. They're likely the ones they want us to find, to keep us nervous, but I'm sure there aren't any others. Why do you think that is?'

'Why use a bug when you have an informer, or an undercover agent in the ranks?'

'Go to the top of the class. You look a bit angry, son. What's goin on?'

Lee ignored the question. 'You know who it is? The informer?'

'No, we don't. Strangely enough, it doesn't really matter. We know who it isn't, which is the important thing.'

Lee got out a cigarette and Kinslow nodded him toward the door. 'The ink and whatnot is pretty flammable.'

'What do you want?' Lee asked.

Kinslow looked hard at Lee. 'I got a warning. A personal call from Greg Downs.'

'His calls would be monitored, wouldn't they?'

'No. Not at Fremantle Prison. He gets his calls, like everyone else.'

It was a stupid question to ask, but Lee had wanted to delay, to allow the news to sink in. 'Does he know where I am?'

'Yes. His lawyer received a call from an anonymous source.'

'One of your boys. Robbie, would be my guess.'

'Yeah, most likely.'

'What did you say?'

Kinslow looked onto the empty lot, all his trucks out on the streets. 'That's not the right question.'

'Alright, what did he offer?'

Kinslow sniffed, spat out the door, thought about it for a long time. 'I told you that I knew your father, in Nam.'

'Yeah, you did.'

'He talk about what happened up there?'

'Hardly at all. Just how much he missed my mother. What he learned about the resilience of the Asiatic races.'

Kinslow's smile was mirthless. 'Yeah, we all learned about that, sure enough.'

'What then?'

'What he's doing now – locked away somewhere, ratting on his mates. It's not the first time.'

Lee controlled his breathing, ironed his hands on the seams of his trousers.

'He might've told you what we did to Vietcong prisoners. And what we wouldn't do, we handed over to the South Vietnamese to do, or the Americans. The commies, in turn, tended not to take us prisoners either. We knew that if we ever got caught, we were dead. It was a great motivator, I can tell you.'

'There were no Australian POWs in Vietnam.'

'You read that in a book?'

It was true. Lee'd read every damn thing he could on the war.

'Officially, that's correct. There's still a few MIA, and that's what your father was, for four months. I wasn't there when it happened. He was on a long-range patrol, got in trouble, it happened all the time. But for some reason, that day the US artillery didn't come pounding in like usual. A chopper was sent in for a very hot extraction. Your father was last seen hanging from a rope, presumed shot, because he fell back into the jungle, a drop of thirty feet. There was heavy fire, heavy rain, and he was left behind. No trace of him when they went back with a full company and APCs the next day. Then, four months later, he comes wandering out of the bush, naked as the day he was born. Long hair and beard. Thinned out and sick, but not a scratch on him.'

Kinslow paused, licked his lips, spat again into the lot. 'I was a junior officer in Intelligence, son, fresh out of Duntroon. Not directly involved with the debrief, but well aware.'

'Aware of what?'

Lee's voice, too harsh – to mask his desire to know.

'Like I say, the commies weren't in the habit of taking Aussie prisoners. Your father, he was a mess. Mentally, I mean. Physically, he was malnourished, but there were no signs of torture. He claimed that he'd been taken up north, forced march. Stuck in a Cambodian pig pen. Questioned by English-speaking NVA officers. Treated like a dog, for two months. As SAS, he was a valuable source of information. Said he tried to kill himself with a stick, but most of the time he was bound to a post. Then he escaped, made his way back south, living off the land, keeping away from people.'

'Get to it. What are you trying to say?'

'I saw the report, son. It was regarded as a counter-intelligence interrogation. Went on for weeks, over there in Vung Tau, on the RAAF base.'

'You saying that he talked, and the North Vietnamese let him go?'

'No chance of that. The report suggested that the likely outcome was that he talked, and got himself better conditions. Conditions that enabled the *possibility* of escape.'

Lee couldn't help himself. His fists were clenched. His face burning.

'Ease up, son. What you got to understand is that while SAS troopers were trained to resist interrogation, every man has a breaking point. Nobody really blamed your father, if he did talk. Like every other soldier, he wasn't privy to operational matters. He went on patrol and did his job. There were no obvious incursions in the following months that suggested heightened intelligence of our operations. Nothing like that.'

'Then what's the point of telling me this? What does it prove?'

Kinslow angled his head, weighing it up. 'Your father was a broken man. My feeling is that he probably told the truth to the best of his recollection. But there was something broke in his head, something he wasn't looking at, or admitting to.

And so he wasn't trusted to go in the field again. He was kept segregated from every other serving man. That was his last tour. He spent the rest of his time, six weeks in country, under observation in a hospital. He was watched, very closely, just in case. There was a diagnosis made, if you're interested, by one of the trick cyclists there. Why he got a medical discharge.'

'He got a medical discharge because he was wounded. I seen the scars.'

'That was self-inflicted, son. In the hospital. He was convinced that he had bullets inside him. He got himself a scalpel and went to town.'

Lee felt sick in his stomach. There were tears starting in his eyes. He couldn't let Kinslow see. 'You're trying to isolate me from my father.'

'I understand why you'd think that, but it ain't it. Not at all. Greg Downs wants me to hand you over. We ain't about to do that, not as long as you're with us. So his men are here, in the city, looking for you. I wanted you to know. To keep away from the depot, where they'll likely be looking. But that you can come to me, if you ever need help. Whatever anybody else says.'

'I don't care about the Knights. And I saw him, last night. My *father*.'

Kinslow looked genuinely surprised, but only for a moment. 'And what was your reading of him – the state of him?'

Kinslow stared hard, and Lee stared back. Kinslow knew the answer to his question.

'Take this any way you like,' Lee said. 'If you don't give Greg Downs and the others what they want, they'll come and take it from you. They'll turn this depot into a bomb crater. You think Robbie would've told them where Frankie lives?'

'Not even Robbie's that stupid. Frankie's ... special. Any hurt came on her, Robbie knows that he'd be dead.'

Kinslow had only answered half of Lee's statement. The part about the Knights taking what they wanted from him, unanswered. Which might mean that they'd come to some kind of arrangement.

'You just focus on your father, and the court case. The Attorney-General's got a big stiffie for the Knights, which is why they've brought the trial forward. Case like this, normally it'd take months to come to trial. But I guess they're happy with what your father's given them, in exchange for his freedom. I were you, I'd wait until after the formalities, which by the look of it won't take long. In the meantime, keep your head down and do what you're told. I hear you've been doing good. Keep it up. We got an election to run. Whatever the outcome, then the big push.'

Kinslow thrust out his paw and Lee shook it. Both men glanced across the lot to see if anyone was looking. Kinslow scouting for the law, and Lee the outlaw.

16.

Lee lost all motivation to get out on the road and earn. There was only one thing on his mind, which was to return to Frankie's for a knock of the hammer to dampen the anger he felt at Brad, and now Kinslow. Were his father's stories all bullshit? Lee hadn't told the truth to Kinslow, out of habit. His father had in fact talked at length about Vietnam, which was the spur that made Lee want to know more, and get books out of the library. His father wasn't welcome at the local RSL, after some dispute years ago, and he wondered now if that was because of his being captured, and his mental breakdown. Which he didn't know was true, either.

He had no reason to trust Kinslow over his father.

Lee found a vein in the back of his wrist and sent the plunger home. He didn't get the old rush of euphoria, but instead an instant sense of gravity that pulled him down onto Frankie's bed.

Most of his father's stories were of stalking the rubber plantations and skirting the edges of rice paddies, watching and waiting. He described the things you could eat in the jungle: the channel catfish in the small streams that could be killed with a rock. The swamp eels with their scaly, snake-like skin, blunt snouts and beady eyes, which breathed air and crawled over land. The larvae in the rotting trunks. Bamboo shoots and turtles. Fungi and algae.

SAS troopers had their dry rations but supplemented where they could. His father spent plenty of time explaining to Lee how they made hoochies in the jungles out of local fern, if possible on a terrace hacked into a hillside, so that they could roll out of bed and be away.

They never lit fires or smoked. They used sign language. They buried everything. They had been told that white men had a pungent smell. After a few days on patrol they concealed their body odour by scouring their armpits with mud. They were supposed to be invisible. To observe and report back. To call in hellfire on the positions they were observing. To track and wait for reinforcements.

But they were not immune to detection. On occasions they were themselves tracked, or observed by hostile villagers. One of Lee's father's best mates, a young corporal from Townsville, fell into a concealed pit that was lined with shit-smeared stakes. He was staked through the belly and groin and Lee's father had to climb down into the pit and smother the man's screams until they could administer morphine and staunch the bleeding. The young corporal died during the extraction of the stake from his groin, rupturing an artery. They held him down as they tried to find the artery with forceps, to pinch off its end, but the wound was deep and he bled out in minutes. Lee's father threw him on his back and fireman-carried him three kilometres to the nearest LZ.

Then there were the firefights and the long nights when the four troopers would sit in the darkness, knowing they were being tracked. The jungle raucous with insect life and the foot pads of animals and men. Rain always a blessing, allowing them to move. There were the days spent camped next to a suspected munitions trail, Claymore mines angled out from the base of trees, scissor legs planted in the dirt, the seven hundred ball bearings aimed in enfilade down the track. When detonated, everything within a hundred yards and less than two metres tall was shredded in a blasting of white noise and black percussion. They liked to fire the mine at mid-range, in case the boxes humped by the VC contained explosives. Upon detonation, the human form was turned into a red mist that hung in the air as long as the noise reverberated through the forest, settling like frost smoke onto the smashed ground.

There were occasional stories that Lee's father told more than once, but there weren't many. He talked about the concealed pit, and holding his friend's mouth while he bled out, the Vietcong company they were tracking only a few hundred metres to their north. The dying man understood, gritted his teeth and tried to stay quiet.

He never told Lee the man's name.

Jack Southern did tell Lee about one Claymore ambush on a jungle trail that led into a rubber plantation near Nui Dat.

Lee's father held the clacker that was joined to the firing wire that was fixed to the detonator cap, which unleashed a wall of angry metal on a dozen male and female Vietcong irregulars in black pyjamas. They were thought to have scouted the Australian base. After the familiar explosion and shower of dirt there was only the wet sound of the soaked rainforest and the watery bodies that were atomised.

Lee's father got a strange light in his eyes when he told these stories, even as his voice became uncharacteristically quiet. They sat around the campfire, Lee stoking the fire and dropping sandalwood sticks onto the coals because that kept his father calm, reminding him that he was at home and safe on his own country, where he was no longer a hunter and no longer being hunted.

He had used those exact words.

They didn't mean much to Lee at the time, but they meant something now.

If what Kinslow said was true, parts of Lee's father had never returned home. Parts of him were still up there, surviving on the land, being interrogated and tortured, hunting and being hunted. Killing, and getting ready to be killed.

What he was preparing for, back here.

When it all came home.

It explained a lot about how they'd lived.

The front door opened and a shadow crossed the jamb of Frankie's door. It was Brad. He held up a flashlight and a balaclava. When Lee didn't move, Brad shone the light over his face, and his works on the bedside table. Then he shone the torch directly into Lee's eyes, reassured by what he saw.

'How'd you deal with the chogie?'

'I took him home. He's not gonna talk.' Lee trying to keep his voice even, to disguise the hatred he felt. They could get to his father, he'd seen that now.

'It's not another visit with your dad, if that's what you're wondering. Get dressed. We got a job. Something new.'

Lee turned on the bedside light. He stared at Brad, reading him for hidden motivations. They'd never done a job at night before. Brad's mouth was sucked in, eyes bulging. He started working his jaw and Lee understood that he was high again. After what Brad had done last night, that meant nothing was certain. His shoulders were hunched like a fighting cat.

Brad closed his eyes to calm himself, cracked his wrists. Then nothing but the sound of his whistling breath. 'I know what you're thinkin, but you don't have a choice. You know that we got access to him, right? You know what that means, right, if you aren't useful?'

'*He's* useful to you in some way. What you need me for?'

'You're useful to us, too, kid. You've done good work these past weeks. You done him proud.'

'I guess that's why he told me to run.'

Brad stood over him, but not too close. 'You don't want to do that, son. That would be a big mistake. There are things that we can do to make your father's life good, and there are ways to make him suffer. I can't say it any plainer than that.'

'I want to see him again.'

'I'll see what I can do. But get your arse into gear. We don't have a lot of time.'

Lee watched Brad's face. Behind the anger was the same burning hatred that he too felt. It had always been there, but hidden. Lee thought again about Kinslow and the Knights, and what arrangements might've been made.

They were using Lee to bargain with his father. They were using his father to bargain with Lee. But what did they want from them? From his father, most likely, his weaponry connection. But from Lee?

'Sure. Give me five.'

17.

Brad was driving a stolen Mazda shitbox, making the right moves with his signals, keeping under the limit. They were driving west toward Fremantle on Canning Highway, the scent of wet grass on the wind, the seaweed smell of the nearby river. Brad looked at his watch and turned on the radio, set to 6PR. They hadn't spoken since leaving the house.

'I don't get you, kid. Most of the fellas that come to the movement are lookin for the brothers and fathers they never had, and the rest of 'em are lookin for a regular opportunity to fight. But you. What do you believe in? What are you planning on doin with your life, when we got this happenin –'

Brad stopped himself at the sound of Kinslow's name, there on the radio, being introduced by Howard Sattler.

'Holy shit. Turn it up.'

Lee did as asked. Kinslow sounded comfortable and confident. He thanked Sattler for the opportunity to get his point across, introducing himself as the leader of the APM and candidate in the forthcoming election.

'This has never happened before, Lee. This is big.'

Lee was still thinking about Brad's question, and what he believed in.

No good answer to that question.

He kept picturing his father, in his isolation cell, coming off the gear. The suffering and desperation.

Lee had always believed what his father believed, but now he wasn't sure what that was.

Kinslow was warming to the task of fending off Sattler's interruptions. Right there, on the airwaves, carried on the warm evening wind across the city, like a patient and warm-hearted guest, Kinslow's deep and reasonable voice began laying out the future of the movement. 'Well, yes, Howard, I do call myself a national socialist. With an emphasis on both the national *and* the socialist. Globalisation has diminished national sovereignty, empowering transnational corporations who don't care about people, disempowering our elected governments. Only a national socialist government in Western Australia will genuinely care for the interests of the West Australian people, because we're the only voices speaking against global capital and the power of banks –'

'But you advocate the overthrow of our democratically elected government, you're demanding –'

'We're not demanding anything, Howard. We're registered as a political party. We're participating in democracy. But let me tell you this. What we have now isn't democracy. What we have is politics, and politicians acting on behalf of vested interests, with a mind only to getting re-elected. What we have is the illusion of democracy, and the most illusory thing of all is when your politicians tell you that they can keep you safe, because they can't keep you safe. Because this is no longer a nation. This is a market. This is a pool of docile consumers. What this country needs, going forward, is not politicians, but leaders.'

'By that you mean white leaders, and white citizens.'

'That's correct. You see, Howard, the health of global capitalism depends upon unending growth, and most of all upon population growth. Free-market capitalism's future therefore assumes a brown world. Whites are the only ones on the planet responsibly managing their populations. The horse has already bolted for the browns and the yellows and the blacks. With population decline in the West, capitalism will demand immigration from brown countries to top up white populations, to keep up economic growth. And then there is the corruption and the mismanagement of all the countries outside of the West. Theft and ineptitude on a grand scale. This creates instability, warfare and competing for scarce resources. You already see it in the countries bordering Europe and North America. Overpopulation. Poverty. Misery. It's just common sense that tells you that one day Europe will be overrun, and America will be overrun, because they're unwilling to secure their borders. It happened to the Roman Empire when they lost control of their borders, and the same will happen again. It's not a pretty picture, our future, Howard, if we allow the status quo to continue. The world will continue to be trashed to benefit a wealthy few.

But we are an island, with borders that can be secured. We have an opportunity to save ourselves, and look to our native capacity to organise and adapt and invent, planning for a safe, viable and sustainable future –'

'And how exactly do you plan to realise that, when –'

'Thank you for that question, Howard, I was just getting to that. What we are proposing is for Western Australia to secede, and to be born again as a white republic, before it's too late. We have the resources to do this. We have the land to sustain us. Those who are unwilling or unwelcome in the new republic can migrate over East, which is already lost. We would invite displaced whites from elsewhere in the world to join us, much like Zionist Israel has done with Jews. We can build something that is new, but is at the same time very old, harking back to when Europe was Europe, when Europe was white. We will be rich, we will be proud, we will be strong –'

'Sounds like a fairytale to me. And in the meantime, you terrorise Asians who live here, minding their own business, getting on with it.'

'We don't condone the attacks, Howard, but at the same time, we didn't ask our elected governments to invite Asians here. They weren't elected to do that. Leaving this aside, it's important to state that we aren't racists. We don't hate those that are different. On the contrary, we respect their difference, and ask that ours too be respected. We are builders and inventors, not destroyers. Our greatest enemies are not Asians, you see, but the self-hating whites who want to bring about the apocalypse of their own culture, by degree, and all so that capitalism can grow and grow, so that a few men get rich while the world goes to hell.'

Brad's lighter flared and for a moment his eyes were bright with a stunned awe. He punched Lee on the shoulder, puffed on his cigarette, grinning. 'This is how it starts, young'un. It's exactly what we've planned for. We get a voice, we win a few votes, and then the major parties shit themselves. Then the whole fucken thing moves to the right, while we keep working, from the inside this time. Fucken eh!'

Brad turned off the radio, ducking his eyes to look down a side street. They were near the port. Lee could smell the sheep piss on the breeze. A golden light settled above the great cranes and container ships beyond the nearest limestone bluff. Brad turned into a street of small office buildings and storage sheds and killed his lights, slowed and checked the numbers written on the kerbs.

*

Lee stood inside the glass door of the building. It was dark but he could see the stray beams of Brad's torch play against the venetians on the second floor. It was a straight B&E and there weren't any security cameras, and no audible alarm had sounded. Brad had carried a bag of tools upstairs with him, and said that he'd be gone a while. They could communicate by walkie-talkie if needed. If a security guard came, Lee had permission to fire a warning shot with the Luger.

There was no escape route except down the same alley they'd entered. A high brick wall circled the lot. He could hear Brad hacking at gyprock upstairs, and then the whine of a drill. A stray cat walked the fenceline next to Lee, until it saw him and leapt out of view. Brad was banging away now with what sounded like a rubber mallet. The subdued thuds echoed around the parking lot, trapped by the high walls.

The sound of Brad's banging was loud, and Lee shut the door to keep the noise down. Once he was inside, it seemed natural to go further. He crept up the stairs and peered into the office where Brad knelt, prying out a floor safe with a crowbar, hammering it with the mallet to get force behind the lever. Lee stepped back and caught the name on the office door. *Dennis Monahan – WA Branch Secretary*. Lee looked down the hall – saw the outlaw Eureka flag on a wooden pole, lit by the streetlights outside, the Maritime Union logo on the board behind.

He backtracked down the stairs. Opened the door and looked into the night. The cat was crouched in the corner of the lot next to a pile of flattened boxes and loose rubbish, swishing its tail and looking at him hatefully. The sound of rats squealing inside the boxes.

Lee turned at the crashing on the stairs. The fold-up trolley that Brad was using to bring down the safe wasn't strong enough; one of its wheels had broken, and Brad was dragging it step by step. Lee propped the door open and went to help. The stairs were narrow and he let Brad take the higher end. Lee took the greater weight, walking backwards toward the door. It wasn't as heavy as he'd expected, but was awkward enough. He felt sharp pains in his knees and lower back, the sinews in his shoulders and neck straining.

They put it down behind the stolen car and Brad opened the boot. They took up the safe again and swung it and dropped, the old shock absorbers lurching. Lee got in the sedan beside Brad and they cruised out of the lot and into the alley. Down at the harbour, a ship's horn blew and the noise made the windows shake. Neither of them spoke. Lee passed Brad a cigarette, and Brad nodded, peeling off his gloves as he drove, knocking off the cement dust in little clouds that settled on his lap.

18.

The normal course of events after a job was Brad asking Lee to head back to his Nollamara house to wind down with booze and goey. Lee's mind was always on hitting Frankie's bed and putting some peacefulness up his arm.

'Yeah, I'll come along with you.'

Brad looked surprised, and then wary.

'Always wondered about safes, and how to get into 'em.'

That made sense to Brad. After all, he'd been mentoring Lee toward a career in armed robbery – said that he had the nerve and the smarts. Not something that went together too often with crims.

'Good boy. We'll get it out of the way and then party. No torturin slopes again, I promise. I'll admit that was my mistake, got carried away.'

Lee wasn't listening. The truth was, he wanted to know what was inside the safe. Brad knew, but he wasn't telling.

Brad drove the sedan over the Fremantle Bridge and headed south past the cemetery, turning into an industrial area of darkened factories, mechanics' workshops and vacant lots whose sandy wastes were populated by stands of wild fennel. The moon was swollen and close, laying pale angles and deep shadows over the headstones in the cemetery.

Brad pulled into the limestone driveway of a wreckers' yard. He passed Lee a keychain and nodded to the iron gate. Lee climbed into the cooling air and found the key and put it into the padlock. He followed Brad through the car graveyard, an acre of car bodies and engines on jarrah blocks, pulling into the open bay of a cement shed where forklifts and dozers slept in the darkness.

*

It was a good safe. Inside the shed lit with banks of bright fluorescent rods they worked on the safe with steel-cutting oxyacetylene, wearing the visors and asbestos-fibre gloves, but barely troubled the safe's annealed sides or titanium door.

It was Lee's idea to get the dozer on the job. He drove the dozer over to the safe and, at regular signals from Brad, dropped the one-tonne blade onto the side of the safe. There was just enough height over the safe to get some gravity working, and the sound was deafening in the confined concrete space.

Five smashes, and Brad shook his head. Lee got out of the cab and looked at the concrete floor underneath the safe, which was beginning to spider-crack.

'I've got some C-4 at home.'

Lee shook his head. 'Don't reckon that'll work any better.

I'll keep trying.'

Two more smashes with the blade and Brad put up a hand. 'I heard something. Them rods might've broke.'

Another smash and even Lee heard the rattle. He reversed the dozer back into its bay and walked to the safe. Brad was working the crowbar inside the fractured doorjamb. He pulled the tool and spat on the floor. 'Get one of them forklifts. Put the safe into the dozer tray and let's see if we can't force the issue.'

Lee did as he was told. He picked up the safe with the twin forks and carried it over to the dozer blade, and placed it on its side. He narrowed the forks and pushed the safe hard against the immovable steel wall. Reversed and slammed forward. Did it again and again until he heard the rods break and then the lock and Brad put up his hand.

Brad drew out the sheaves of papers and manila folders, a Filofax and a cigar-box filled with mini-cassette tapes. Some maps and a couple of glue-bound documents. A handgun in a black canvas holster. A box of ammo.

Brad ran his hands around the safe's insides until he was sure it was empty. 'Just leave all the broken stuff here. This is one of Kinslow's businesses.'

He flicked through a couple of the folders. Glossy colour photographs and grainy black and whites. Faces and naked bodies. 'Oh, this is fucken grouse.'

Brad surprised Lee by passing him the folder. 'Monahan, and every branch secretary like him, or corporate CEO with any brains, use politics to get what they want, and when that fails, they use a private investigator.'

'Is this …?'

Lee could hardly believe it.

'Yeah, it's the Premier, back before he was the Premier. Others helped put him there, in the big seat, but they can just as easy take it away. How it works, kid. And now we got this stuff – dirt going back generations – we can make it work for us. This cache is the stuff of rumours. I've heard there's judges, pollies, rich bastards left, right and centre. So far, the big wheels of this town, they ain't scared of us. They got the power to crush us with their blue uniformed stooges. But *these* bastards only care about their reputations, their snouts in the trough. This shit is better than a thousand armed men.'

The Premier's face stared up at Lee, his eyes blurry with desire, the milky light over his head enough to cast into sharp relief the object of his attention, her breasts and belly and wet black triangle, her eyes looking directly at the camera. Lee flicked through the folder. Other faces he recognised. Transcripts of conversations referenced to tape recordings.

And this just one of the folders.

'This is incredible. How'd you know where to look?'

Brad glanced up and smiled, saw behind the question, but for whatever reason decided to play. 'Some MUA mutt got arrested for GBH, fell out with the leadership. He was looking at losing his job as a crane driver, so he called Kinslow, an old employer of his. We got him the best legal representation and he got off. Let's roll out, young fella. I got to drop these somewhere and we can call it a night.'

Brad's smile genuine, but his eyes giving him away, watching to see if Lee would take anything. Lee closed the folder and handed it back, Brad nodding. 'Good man. You don't want to be in possession of this stuff. Not unless you want a slow, painful death.'

They walked to the car, laden with the files and boxes. The moon was high, the car bodies massed in every direction.

*

To get to the rented garage in the brick-paved lane they had to drive past the depot. Dawn was coming, a rim of purple light over the range that rose above the city like a great dark wave, poised eternally.

Osborne Park was quiet except for the occasional security vehicle doing the rounds of the warehouses and factories surrounding the lake. The depot was locked and dark, the towing rigs parked against a brick wall. Because there was an informer in the APM ranks, Lee assumed that there was no need for the coppers to maintain an overnight surveillance of the depot, but there was the regulation Falcon sedan, parked across the street beside a stand of paperbark. Except that the nearest streetlight illuminated the face of the man in the car, head tilted back and eyes closed.

Lee didn't say anything, but he must've flinched, or given some other sign, because Brad sped up and drove past the garage alley. 'What is it?'

'That wasn't a copper. I know him. He's a Knights prospect. Name of Danny Hislop.'

'Alright then. He see you?'

'He was dozing. I think.'

Brad turned to circle the block. They were out of sight of the Falcon, but he was making sure. 'If he's a Knight, not a copper, then he won't be alone. Unless he thinks he can take you himself.'

'He doesn't think that.'

'We can't drive past again. It's too obvious.'

Brad pulled over, scanned the lake for early morning joggers or dog walkers. 'When was the last time you spoke to Kinslow? Here, I mean.'

'This afternoon. I came and filled up, and we had a cigarette and a chat. He told me to stay away.'

'You see anyone then?'

'No.'

Brad started the car and they circled round and drove into the brick-paved alley, parked in front of garage number seven. 'Wait here.'

Brad unlocked a roller door and scrolled it up, revealing a dark empty room, a single electrical cable threaded around jarrah joists, a naked bulb. A giant safe stood against the far wall. Brad popped the boot and carried in the boxes of files. Knelt and worked the combination, opened the safe and stowed the files away, closed the safe door and spun the lock.

Brad got back in the car, lit a cigarette, mulled it over.

'If there's one, and they want to take you, there'll be more.'

'Yeah, there will.'

'Better we deal with it here, than elsewhere.'

Brad reached under the driver's seat and drew out a tyre iron. 'Normally, I have my katana, but not tonight. This'll work. You know these guys. This is your operation. What degree of force?'

Lee thought about what he could say, should say. Hislop would want to kill him, but the others would want to hold him, until the court case.

'Frighteners,' Lee answered.

'Wrong call.'

'We don't have the numbers to drag them away somewhere else.'

Brad didn't like it. He drew hard on his cigarette, flicked it out the window. 'We could *draw* them away, to somewhere quiet.'

'Numbers.'

Brad nodded. 'So we leave them out here, holding their dicks. But I'll need to get my orders. I don't like this at all. With the election coming, these yokels could fuck it all up. Let's head.'

Brad drove through the alley and turned toward the lake. Hislop was still dozing, his chin tilted back, stubble on his jawline. Even so, Lee ducked as they passed, Brad caressing the tyre iron. 'Lucky man, Sleeping Beauty. You're a lucky, lucky, man.'

Lee started to rise and Brad held him down. 'There's the rest of 'em.'

Brad took his hand off Lee's shoulder, who looked in the wing mirror at the black Ford van, windows painted over, parked in the shadows near the lake.

Lee thinking about Brad's hand on his shoulder, like they were friends. Thinking, the enemy of my enemy …

19.

Two days before Jack Southern's court appearance, the details of the trial went front-page news. Three journos on the byline was a signal, according to Frankie, that the journalists were scared of repercussions. Lee read the article in the backyard, smoking and drinking coffee, a family of magpies carolling in the marri branches, the afternoon soft and vivid. Frankie was inside doing her washing, getting ready for her shift.

Lee had been following her the past week. He was shooting up four or five times a day now, and that was just to stay square. With his father due to be released, he didn't want to be caught out. Frankie had a fresh gram every morning when she returned from work. The early hour made him assume that she picked up the gram on her way to work, rather than after her shift. He wanted to find her dealer, and make his own deal.

He'd been ordered to stay indoors, to avoid running into the small group of Knights who were looking for him, staking out the depot and the courthouse. He obeyed for a few days, lying in his bed, on the gear and thinking about his father up there in Vietnam. Had he experienced a reality that nobody was willing to consider, as he described it? Or was Jack Southern so damaged that he didn't know the difference between what was real, and what was in his head?

Lee didn't know, and he quit the house and began working the highways during the day, saving his money. He was getting between five and ten tows a day, paid in cash. When his father was released they'd have to run wide and far. Several of the Knights were long-haul truckies that visited every part of the state, and there'd be nowhere safe to hide.

In the meantime, he was also saving so that he could buy Emma a car. She had half the money she needed, and he aimed to surprise her and pitch in the other half, as a goodbye present. She wanted an old Beetle, and he'd been keeping an eye on the auctions and the car yards he passed every day, and the second-hand adverts in the Thursday paper. He'd even gone and looked at a couple. Found one '78 model with a custom green paint job and leather upholstery; however, its engine knocked and its exhaust was black. One glare at the owner, a Pommy retiree, and he'd known to leave it alone.

Aware that he was leaving, Lee tried to see Emma once a day, always after school. He gave the excuse of saying he'd driven up from Albany to see a friend in Freo Prison, and was staying with his family. She didn't ask who.

They hadn't gotten together again, but it was moving toward that. She held onto him when they walked through Fremantle, stopping at the markets, and she kissed him when they parted. He hadn't raised the idea of taking her south for a weekend. He thought about it, but every time he saw their reflection in a shop window he knew that their futures were going to be different.

*

Lee's plan was to buy himself a few grams from Frankie's dealer, to ease himself off when he ran. Each time he shadowed Frankie in her red Mini Cooper, she drove to the same house. It wasn't the kind of house he expected; not a rundown flat in an outer area, but rather a riverside mansion in a wealthy suburb. He kept his distance behind her, but he was close enough to see that she had her own electronic key. The key opened a sliding gate that gave off to a concrete drive sloping down to the river. Security cameras on the gate and on the wall. Two black Doberman guard dogs with cut ears and cropped tails, following her car at a trot.

Lee had thought to ask one of the old boys at the boxing gym. The white guy, Frank, said he was a private investigator. Had once been a cop. Perhaps he could find out who lived at the mansion. But it was the other guy, Gerry, who was at the gym most days. He sparred with Lee in the makeshift ring, building Lee's fitness and speed and in particular teaching him the art of counter-punching. Gerry reckoned that Lee had the talent to make himself a name, but Lee suspected it was just the old boy recognising that he was in trouble – the evidence being the track marks on his arms and the fury that escaped him in the ring – Gerry parrying until the storm had passed.

Today's front page had a picture of Lee's father, with his eyes blacked out, standing alongside Greg Downs in their full camo gear with Armalite rifles. Lee knew that it was his father because Lee had taken the photo, wasn't sure how the press got hold of it.

The identity of the 'supergrass' was still a secret. There was no suggestion that the man beside Greg Downs was the turncoat. Instead, the focus of the article was on the automatic weaponry. The Armalite was the US infantry regulation rifle, and there were questions about how many the Knights had in their possession, and where they'd been sourced. What other banned weapons were part of their armoury.

The rest of the article outlined the rise of the revolution-ary right in Australia – evidenced by the recent firebombing of Asian businesses in our own streets. Fears of shared intelligence and arms dealing. The Knights regarded as little more than a symptom of a wider malaise. Not much of a threat, according to unnamed sources. Product of small minds in a small country town.

Red rag to a bull, Lee thought.

He could imagine his father reading the same article. Everything he'd worked for, a bit of a joke.

But there was truth to it, when viewed from a distance.

Lee hoped his father saw that.

*

Brad pulled up in the drive. Another stolen car – this time a battered Landcruiser. He flashed his lights and Lee locked the house door. It was a warm night and the moon hadn't risen. There were a surprising number of stars in the sky: he could see Venus, Mars on the horizon, the Saucepan and the Southern Cross. The bright swathe of the Milky Way, billions of stars roaring behind a million years of silence.

Brad passed Lee a balaclava and a pair of soft leather gloves.

'You see the front page?' he asked, cranking up the Landcruiser, waiting for the engine to settle from its hard rocking before he put her in reverse.

'Yeah, I saw it.'

'Don't take that shit to heart, kid. The media always does that – it's their job. Paint us as fools and loonies. They'd shit their pants if they knew how many soldiers, coppers and screws support our cause. Better they don't know, until the time comes.'

'That's what I figured.'

Brad was on the speed again, his ropy forearms clenching and unclenching, his hands white on the wheel.

'What's the job tonight?'

Brad grinned. 'Need-to-know basis, son.'

'You don't reckon I need to know?'

'Nah, I don't. The same as before. You're on cocky duty while I do the hard yards. This place isn't like the others. There's going to be security. One guy parked outside the house. Full-time, the poor bastard.'

Brad clearly wanted him to ask, to cajole until he learned more, but Lee wasn't in the mood.

*

They parked on the buffalo grass verge of a house that was hidden behind a high, stuccoed wall. Beneath them, the warm salty smell of the river rose over the blocks of mansions, the smeary lights of the city further east. Lee knew his way around the suburbs now. This was Peppermint Grove, the richest in the state, on the leeside of the hills that fronted the windy coast. The air was humid with condensation from all the lush gardens.

Brad didn't open the back of the car. Didn't carry a bag of heavy tools. Like Lee, he wore a balaclava and gloves, was dressed in dark overalls and black tennis shoes.

He drew out a hunting knife with a serrated blade from inside his overalls and then a black pistol and something else black. It was a suppressor, the first Lee had ever seen. Brad passed Lee the knife while he screwed the suppressor onto the pistol barrel.

'This ain't the neighbourhood for people to own junkyard dogs, but just in case.'

Brad stowed the knife and the silenced pistol in his overalls. He nodded to the wall, indicating for Lee to hoist him up. Lee made a saddle of his hands and took his weight. Brad rolled and dropped over the wall, and Lee leapt and pulled himself up.

On the other side of the wall was a blue-tiled swimming pool that reflected the starlight, and a series of stepped gardens full of tropical plants that mostly concealed the glass wall at the back of the house. Lee dusted off his trousers but Brad indicated with the pistol that they skirt the pool. He stowed the pistol and lifted his foot for Lee to hoist him over the next wall. They climbed and crossed three backyards before Brad crouched and knelt and checked the suppressor on the barrel.

They were in a large yard with another swimming pool lit from within. Leaves floated on its surface. There was a gazebo with a shingle roof between the pool and the large house built in the style of a station homestead, with deep shadowy verandas and a tin roof. Faint strains of classical music coming from the second floor. The ground floor was dark and quiet. No sign of a dog, although Brad didn't pack away his gun. Lee followed Brad as he skirted the side wall and entered the veranda and knelt beside the back door. He pushed the door with his gloved hand, and it clicked. He took out a slim jim and worked it between door and jamb until there was a secondary click. Now he rose and opened the door, took Lee by the shoulder and drew him through the cool darkness of the wood-panelled hall that led to the front door. From their position by the front door they could see down a garden path to a man parked in a Ford LTD, reading a newspaper by torchlight. Brad shook Lee's shoulder and used his forked fingers to indicate that Lee needed to watch the man in the car. Lee stood and leaned against the wall that smelled like fresh paint. From the dining room came the remnant smells of roast lamb.

The man in the car kept reading, and Lee continued watching him. He was in some kind of uniform. On the dash was the formal hat that navy captains wear.

Lee looked around the hall for something that would

identify the owner of the mansion, but there was only a hatstand with a Crombie cap and a Claremont football scarf. A board of keys with little enamel tags. A painting of an old man with mutton-chops and a photograph of the house that looked like it was taken a hundred years ago. It was too dark to read the steel plaque beneath it.

Brad was only gone for a few minutes. Lee heard the quiet padding of his shoes on the polished floorboards upstairs, then the squeaks on the stairs. He nodded to Lee who checked the driver one final time, now peeling a mandarin.

Lee followed Brad through the rooms. He was behaving strangely, gently tipping over candleholders and vases but being ruthlessly quiet about it. Rummaging through the kitchen drawers, leaving them open. It was when he opened the fridge door that Lee saw the blood sprayed across Brad's overalls. Blood on his gloves and forearms. Blood on his neck and the side of his face. Like it'd been painted with a brush. Like it'd been squirted on him with a syringe. Brad catching Lee's eyes and shaking his head, continuing to disarray the back room, pulling blankets and coats and linen onto the floor, but in perfect silence.

Out in the yard and against the side wall, Brad indicated that Lee should take his weight again.

'What the fuck happened?'

'Shut your mouth. Till we get to the car.'

They went over the four walls, Lee tumbling onto the verge. He'd been calm inside the mansion until he saw the blood. Now his heart was beating fast and his fingers were tingling and his guts were awash with nerves. He climbed into the passenger seat and Brad turned the ignition, which failed to catch. Brad closed his eyes and turned the key again, the starter motor whirring loudly before the spark caught and the engine roared.

Brad left the lights off until they reached the highway. He pulled in behind a kombi full of surfers and headed north and east, the most direct route back to the city. The highway was quiet. Just when Lee was about to speak, Brad raised his hand. There was a police car, parked in the shadows of a vacant school carpark, nose toward them.

They passed the cop car and Brad looked nervously into the rear-vision. He pulled into a side road and zigzagged the suburban streets, heading east.

'You're going to read about this, but we never speak about what just happened, you hear? Tonight's the start of something we've been planning for a while. The start of something big.'

There was a tremble in his voice, whether departing adrenalin or shock, it was hard to tell. Either way, Brad was staring at him, willing him to meet his eyes.

'You hear?'

'Yeah, I hear. Just tell me –'

'I ain't telling you shit. Now, I'm gonna drive this baby up into the hills and torch her, and you … you're gonna go home and plug your arm and dream sweet, you hear me?'

Lee nodded, peeling off his gloves. The roads were quiet, barely a light inside any of the houses. Sprinklers ticked over front lawns. For a moment he'd hoped that the cop car would pull them over, bring everything to an end. He wasn't going to dream sweet tonight.

20.

Lee was still awake when Frankie returned from her shift. She put the fresh gram, wrapped in a *Women's Weekly* page, on the kitchen table. She folded her arms around his shoulders, her hair smelling of perspiration and disinfectant. 'Your father sent word. He wants you to attend court. He doesn't want you to see him in that position, but you got to be there anyway. Regardless of the idiots who're trying to stop you. It's part of the deal.'

'Who told you that?'

The same answer as always. 'Never mind who told me. That's what your father said. I'm just the messenger.'

Lee clipped the mainspring of the Luger to the coupling link lever, clicked the breechblock end piece and the firing pin together, assembled the rest of the parts, working automatically, as he'd been doing these past hours.

'Brad said that what we did, it'd be in the news.'

'Sure you want to see it?'

'Yeah, I am.'

Frankie returned with her works and the newspaper. She passed him the paper and began to make up a solution to share. There it was, on the front page, just like Brad said.

'The Governor?'

Frankie watched him, her eyes hard. 'You think it's too ambitious? Too … grandiose?'

Lee searched for it in her face, but couldn't find it. Doubt. Remorse. Fear.

Everything that he was feeling.

'No', he said quietly. 'I think it's insane.'

Frankie pushed the hair out of her eyes. 'I wouldn't expect you to understand. People like you think that what we're planning is hard to do, or impossible. But it isn't. Nobody is safe from us, and we've shown that. It's part of a strategy; the first step. None of your concern.'

'Then why get me involved? If you don't trust me?'

'I don't want to talk about it,' she replied, rubbing the plunger around the slurry of powder and water. 'And I don't want you to talk about it, either. You've got to keep it together for another couple of days.'

'Is that a threat?'

Frankie snorted, carefully, lest she disturb the air near the open packet. Her movements with the needle and saucer were like Lee's movements assembling the gun.

She passed him his fresh syringe, nothing in her eyes. She drew up her own shot and tapped the syringe and squirted, lifted a bare foot onto her seat and began searching between her toes, hair falling in a curtain over her face.

A tide of nausea found its level in Lee's throat. He could feel the sharpness in his gills, the acid in his mouth. He swallowed and opened his arm, looking for a vein. Slid home the plunger and waited for the blanketing surge to carry him away.

Frankie was looking at him. 'I'm jealous of you. When the books are written, your name will be raised up. You'll be remembered. What you've done, what you've been doing. Whether you're reluctant or not.'

The smack was strong, forced a balance with the shock that unsettled him, became a welcome numbness. Now Lee could read the article. Now he could look beyond the picture of the Governor, smiling beside his wife, cutting the ribbon of a new hospital, his cropped grey hair and winged white eyebrows, his smiling eyes.

A suspected break-in. A spate of robberies nearby over the past weeks. Despite resident complaints. The first governor to live away from Government House. Didn't want the formality or the trappings of power. A country boy who got his law degree through night school. Ended up a High Court judge. A man with the common touch.

The creation of a CIB task force had been announced to investigate the murder. All uniformed and plain-clothes coppers were recalled from leave. Every crim with a history of armed robbery, burglary and petty theft was to be dragged in for questioning. Federal police and ASIO investigations to commence, working in tandem with the local force. The Governor's was a purely ceremonial role as the Queen's representative, but not without its influence. He was the most high-profile murder victim that the state had ever seen.

It was only then that Lee understood. The break-in was never about stealing documents, or anything else for that matter. It was a straight-up assassination, made to look like a robbery gone wrong.

Meaning that nobody would be claiming responsibility.

What then its purpose?

Frankie was on the nod, a sleepy smile on her face. Lee stood, and she stood too.

'I'm gonna shower, then get some sleep. You want to join me?'

Her voice neutral, like they'd been discussing football scores or the weather, and not the murder of the state's most senior public official.

Lee watched her sleepwalk down the hall, heard the hiss of the shower, the spatter of water on the tiles. He sat down and lit a cigarette, looked again at the Governor's face, innocent of what was coming for him.

Like us all, he thought.

Lee tried to see a way beyond what was coming for him. Run. Go to the police. The media. Try and explain. But everywhere he looked it ended the same way, with him either locked up or murdered for what he knew, what he had said.

The same thing his father was going through now.

The only man who could tell him what to do, not there to help him.

He thought of her then, for the first time in a long while – his mother. Just the same old image, sepia-toned from wear and repair, Lee holding it in his mind, trying not to change it. His mother leaning over his cot, rubbing Vicks onto his congested chest, singing him a lullaby. The fear he felt at not being able to breathe, the burn of the eucalyptus oil in his nostrils, his watering eyes, the firm pressure of her fingers as they pushed at his bony chest, his soft belly. He listened to the crooning syllables that fell gently from her lips, the loving voice belying sadness; the piece of the picture that was hardest to fix, to hold true: her cut lip and swollen eye, the single teardrop that slid from her good eye, rolling down her nose and falling onto his mouth.

*

Lee spent the morning tuning up the Ford, adjusting the timing by ear and changing the oil and plugs, disassembling the carburettor and changing the gaskets, adjusting the fuel volume with a Phillips-head screwdriver until the engine sounded right. Police helicopters patrolled the skies, coming over the suburb in fifteen-minute intervals. At a nearby army salvage Lee bought a second-hand Vietnam-era swag and hoochie. He bought an air force greatcoat and a thick beanie. A pair of boots and some cheap sunglasses. All in his father's size.

Lee topped up the long-range tanks at the local servo, buying snacks and filling up the plastic water jerries at the tap beside the toilet. Waiting in line to pay for the fuel, he noticed that the two daily newspapers had put out special editions. The man and woman ahead of him in the line talked about the murder, watching as a police cruiser swung through the pumps, both coppers looking at every car. Lee pulled his cap down low. He didn't know whether they were looking for him. Outside, he locked the new gear in the steel box on the Ford's back tray, strapped the jerries to the racks and headed south of the river.

The boxing gym was empty at the rear of the video store. Lee parked the truck out front and walked down the sloping drive with his bag of wraps and Dunlop Volleys. He let himself in with the key and stretched in front of the giant mirrors. He worked his jaw loose where he'd been clenching through the long night. He'd kept himself busy during the day but had felt increasingly sick in his stomach. His limbs were still heavy with the delayed shock of what he'd done, what he'd helped make happen. He put himself through the regime that Gerry had worked out for him, doubling the intensity and duration – the warm-up of stretches, then free weights, then the speedball and floor-to-ceiling, then three-minute rounds on the heavy bag. Because neither Gerry nor Frank was there, he filled in the combinations with side and snap kicks, the sound of his feet making a fierce slap on the leather between the flurries of punches.

When he couldn't stand any longer, Lee sat on his haunches, then lay back on the cold cement. His muscles throbbed and his heart pumped behind the cold thrumming of the hammer in his veins. He closed his eyes and slept.

He awoke with a start. The gym was dark and empty. He didn't know how long he'd been asleep. He showered in the grimy change room and climbed into his jeans and boots.

Outside, he stood in the sun and smoked a cigarette and felt the sunshine dry the skin on his face and shoulders and belly. He put on his best shirt and locked the gym. He left his wraps strung over a pole beside the door. Somebody else could have them.

It was nearly three o'clock and he got stuck in traffic crossing the river. All day he'd avoided turning on the radio, knowing what the lead story and talkback discussion would be turning over, endlessly and repetitively. With the radio silent and the smack in his blood, he tried to pretend that nothing had changed in the world.

He'd made the right decision, but wasn't sure of the order of events. After his father was released, Lee had decided to go to the police with what he knew, but as an anonymous source. The problem was that he didn't have any evidence. There was nothing linking Frankie to the robberies or the murder. He didn't know Brad's real identity, or where the old man lived. Even if Lee turned himself in, there was no guarantee that he'd be believed, or that he wouldn't take the rap alone. He needed proof of what had happened, and there wasn't much time.

*

He got to Emma's school five minutes late. Already the footpaths were crowded with students, chatting and wandering toward the bus stands. Lee parked across the road, let the sea breeze blow through the cab, dappled sunlight playing across his forearms.

It was only when he realised that he might have missed Emma that he understood. Turned the ignition and put the truck in gear. Her father was right – Lee was poison in her life. He was a fool to want to see her, to say goodbye.

One last goodbye – an opportunity to memorise her face and eyes and hair. The sound she made when she laughed, when she feigned anger and teased him.

To hold that in his mind, and not let it fade, as his mother's face had faded.

Lee pulled behind the first bus and saw her, the moment she saw him. She was seated at the back of the bus. She blew him a kiss. Some of her friends looked at her, and then at him. She pointed down the bus, indicating that she'd get off at the next stop, and then stood and pulled the leather strap and staggered out of his vision.

The bus slowed, and pulled in to the kerb.

Lee kept driving, putting his foot down, losing the churning in his guts and the meaning of his tears within the swerving brought about by his hard acceleration. He only slowed when he skidded to avoid colliding with a woman in a Commodore, turning across him, three kids in the back seat. He drove carefully after that, not thinking of anything but letting it build. He reached the Osborne Park depot just as two of the True West tow trucks pulled into the lot. They didn't see him, and he drove further down the street and parked. He walked along the lake's shore with his cap pulled low, then cut back to the road. Danny Hislop was still there, parked in his Falcon, three empty iced-coffee cartons and countless butts tipped into the low gutter. Lee clocked that the door was unlocked and yanked it open and reached for the dash and grabbed the walkie-talkie and flung it behind him. Hislop's seat was reclined, and Lee kept one foot on the street and straddled him like a lover, started laying down forearm blows, choking him with the other wrist against his throat, punch after punch until Hislop's eyes rolled and he went out.

Lee ran his fingers through Danny's pockets and extracted two hundred and forty dollars cash. He took the Smith and Wesson .38 revolver that was at Danny's feet. He kicked the door shut and looked around. Nobody had seen him. He walked back to the lake and tossed in the revolver while five black swans angled out of the western sky, feet extended to brake them as they hit the water and began to glide.

21.

Lee had never seen any building like the Supreme Court. Tall reeded columns dominated the entrance, diminishing even the peacock confidence of the dark-suited lawyers going about their business, hair barbered to white stripes at the backs of their necks.

All the flags throughout the city were flying at half-mast, including the national and state flags of the court.

Lee kept his cap pulled low and his eyes keen. He was unarmed, the Luger locked in his truck, presuming that he'd be searched going into the court. There were no Knights that he could see. Neither was there any visible police presence, every copper out on the streets, making a show of force.

Frankie had told him that the lawyers would jaw through the morning, completing their opening statements. It was after lunch now, and around the time his father was due to be trotted out. Lee's plan was to make himself visible at the back of the courtroom, and then depart. Wait for his father at the rear exit to the courthouse. Hear what his father's next move was. Learn how to get in contact, once his new identity was confirmed. The Ford was parked a block away, in case his father could leave with him.

Lee waited at the foot of the stairs and watched the crowd file into the courtroom. It was musty and hot inside the building and he began to sweat. Still no familiar faces among the crowds. Nobody meeting his eye. Nobody watching him.

Outside the courtroom was a framed picture of the dead Governor, back when he was a Supreme Court judge. A vase of flowers beneath the picture stand. The judge's wig slightly askew, his red robes gathered around the white bib at his throat, a warm smile on his face.

A uniformed arm reached outside the courtroom door and began to pull it shut. Lee slipped through in time. The guard looked him up and down, but there was no search, no metal detector.

The court was packed. Red carpet and yellow walls. Wooden benches lined with men in black robes at the front. A wooden balcony with an open door where the jury sat. Wood panelling behind the judge, looking down at the microphone, a gold-painted crest statue above his head, words in Latin.

An empty balcony to the judge's left.

Lee stood at the back of the courtroom, avoiding the guard's eyes, who was indicating that he should sit with the others in the twenty rows of wooden bench seats.

Now Lee saw them: Danny Hislop and three other Knights, right at the front.

Danny's face, which must be a mess, hidden from view.

Directly in front of them, wearing a dark blue suit, the great bald head of Greg Downs, conferring with his lawyer in whispers.

The judge began a preamble but Lee kept his eyes on Danny Hislop and the others. None of them moved, or talked. They stared ahead, at the judge.

There was a murmur. In the first row before Lee a young man got out a sketchpad and three pencils, put one in his mouth.

'… Jack Brendon Southern.'

Lee's father emerged from behind the door in the wood-panelled wall. He wore the same prison greens, scab of grey beard on his chin. Black bags under his eyes, searching for and finding Lee, blinking and pretending he hadn't seen.

Lee's father focused instead on Hislop and the others, trying for a withering stare, but failing. It'd only been a few days since their meeting in the Canning Vale prison, but his father had deteriorated even more. There was something smaller about him in the presence of the overt symbols of legal power, with his bent head and skinny arms, his gaunt face. The tan gone from his skin, now a pallid grey colour. Shoulders rounded and left hand moving over his right knuckle, repetitively, a slight tremble there.

'State your name for the jury.'

Lee's father straightened his back, tried to project. 'My name is Jack Brendon Southern.'

The supergrass.

The gravel gone from his voice.

More murmuring from the floor.

'Silence, please.'

'And for the jury, Mr Southern, please state your position in the organisation that has been hitherto referred to as the Southern Knights, or the White Knights, or the Knights.'

Lee's father began to ramble. Lee knew that voice. It was the voice at the end, after the week, sometimes eight, nine, ten days of sleeplessness, standing in the hall looking out at the night, rocking on his heels and muttering, awake but asleep, eyes wide shut.

'Thank you, Mr Southern.'

The judge looked pitifully at Lee's father.

Nobody had ever regarded him with that expression.

His father saw it too, opened his jaw wide, blinked, started again on repetitively working his knuckle into the palm of his other hand, as involuntary as the watering of his eyes.

'Mr Southern. We have heard from the Crown Prosecutor that you are prepared to name the person responsible for the homicide of Brady Downs. Do you see that person in the courtroom today?'

'Yes, I do.'

'Then can you please, for the benefit of the jury, point to that person, and address them by name.'

Lee's father said nothing. Leaned forward. Closed his eyes.

'Mr Southern.'

Lee's father raised a trembling finger, but he didn't point it at Greg Downs. He pointed instead at Danny Hislop, gave him a knowing smile before turning back to the judge.

'*I* did it.'

'I beg your pardon? Mr Southern –'

Now he stood. '*I* did it. I murdered Brady Downs!'

Shouts from the floor. The prosecutor stood from his bench. Greg Downs' lawyers recognising what that meant. The judge banging his gavel. Danny Hislop and the Knights, standing as one.

'Be seated!!'

Greg Downs was turned, reaching across the divider to the other Knights, Lee catching the expression on his face, and then, as if in slow motion, Lee saw the gun in Danny Hislop's hand, pointed at his father. Heard Greg Downs' voice, a shriek above the cacophonous shouting, the hardwood walls locking in the swirling sound, punctuated by the banging of the wooden gavel, Downs' shout of 'No! Danny, there's no need –'

But too late.

The familiar percussion and muzzle flame, the echo of the fierce bang.

The screams.

The crowd moving like choppy water, falling over each other to get out of the room.

Danny Hislop charging through them, over them.

Lee's father, slumped in his chair, the rear cushion blown apart where the bullet had passed through his chest.

Lee looked up to see Hislop raising the .38 snubnose, taking aim at him, his blood-red swollen eyes and broken mouth, opening to shout, tackled from behind by a guard, the gun discharging into the carpet. More guards dragging out Lee's father, his green sweatshirt soaked in blood.

22.

The Tactical Response Group arrived in their dark vans, windows blocked out. They corralled the crowd in the forecourt while detectives in tan suits took details from a line of witnesses. Lee watched the rest of the Knights being taken away in a paddy wagon. The television crews darted around the edges, moving from witness to witness, microphones thrust into stunned faces.

Lee walked out of the Supreme Court gardens and skirted the park, re-emerged at the rear of the courthouse that was blocked by a line of police cars and men with shotguns. He wanted to see his father. He wanted to see him alive.

Two ambulances with strobing lights were waiting. The ambulance drivers entered the courthouse with a trolley. The police officers covered the rear exit. Lee thought about what had just happened, and what it meant.

His father had admitted to the murder, but his father had full immunity.

His plan all along, perhaps.

Lee's father couldn't have committed the murder, because he wasn't around when Downs had gone missing. Lee and his father had been out in the bush near Paynes Find, changing water stores and swapping over foodstuffs in an abandoned mine, rappelling down into the red shaft framed with hand-cut boughs of she-oak, checking the ammunition and weapon caches in ten different locations all the way back to Geraldton.

It was something they did every July.

Downs was last seen at a Geraldton nightclub the same night they were camped beside a dry riverbed out near Cue.

Lee had no idea why his father had admitted to the murder, except that he wasn't the kind to settle scores in a courthouse.

Lee smoked a cigarette, his hands trembling.

It was plain to him now – the direct line of stupidity and malice that led to this point.

That he was part of.

Danny Hislop had murdered Emma's cousin, David. Lee had bashed Hislop. Hislop's father had demanded that Lee be excommunicated from the Knights. The Downs brothers had been swayed against it by Lee's father. Brady Downs had died as a result, so that Jack Southern might be framed for the murder. Lee's father had got himself ahead of the curve. Had himself arrested on a weak charge, made deals with whoever he needed to – the state, the APM – to keep himself safe.

And now, what Lee's father had said under oath.

What it meant.

Greg Downs would walk free.

The ambulance medics wheeled out the trolley, down the

ramp and onto the gravel. Lee felt the tension leave him in a hard shudder that started at the base of his spine and finished at the back of his neck. His father was alive. Oxygen mask on his face. Eyes open, blinking, and looking around.

Lee's father would remain in jail, on the existing charge of possession. No new identity for him. They'd throw the book. Whoever had made the immunity deal would need the redress, to save face.

But it wasn't a serious charge. He would be free within the year, either way.

In jail, he'd be vulnerable.

Whatever deal he'd made with the APM for his protection was now broken. He'd betrayed them too.

It was time to run.

*

Lee returned to the Inglewood house to clean out his things, but Frankie was waiting for him at the kitchen table. Still dressed in her scrubs, smiling at him over the rim of a teacup. 'Did you hear on the radio?'

'I was there. It happened right in front of me.'

'No, not that.'

There was a cold light in her eyes. 'I'm talking about the leader of the opposition, John Howard, and the leader of the Nationals, Sinclair. They both said this morning that Australia's getting too Asian. That immigration should be slowed. You know what that means? What we've achieved already? The Labor Prime Minister *has* to come out and respond to them, say that it's good to have Asians walking in and taking over. That's electoral poison. That's a wedge, right there.'

'I didn't hear. But –'

'I'm sorry about your father, I really am. But when you turn rat, you have to expect that kind of thing.'

Lee felt a flush of anger. 'I don't know what my father promised you people, but it's –'

'What do you mean, *us people*?'

Frankie stared coolly at him, but when he didn't answer, she smiled, nodded to the gram packet on the table. His works already there, laid upon the saucer. 'Go on and help yourself. I already made a start. I'm gonna head to the supermarket, get some things.'

Lee took the seat she vacated. He watched her retrieve her car keys from the hook by the front door, exit into the morning light.

He opened the packet and tapped out a pile onto the edge of the saucer. Pushed it across with the nub of the plunger, rubbed it around until it all dissolved.

His last shot, before he hit the road, for good.

The plan was to head north, and live off the stores at his great-grandfather's secret camp. Why he needed his books, before he left.

Hide up there until he could visit his father, in prison.

Lee drew up the clear liquid and raised the syringe to the light. Tapped it and squirted.

He was just about to put it in his arm when he realised that the solution was bubbling.

He laid the syringe down, put his finger to his tongue and dabbed it in the gram packet. Put his finger up to his mouth, but stopped. His fingertip burning with something caustic. He sniffed, and it smelled familiar.

Lee rose and opened the cupboard under the sink. There was the packet of Drano, its spout crusted with powder. He sniffed it and put it back. Now he saw the knife in the sink, powder still on the upper blade where she'd chopped the grains into the finest white powder.

Lee went and looked in his room.

It was cleaned out.

Bed made and sheets changed and pillows puffed with air.

Like he'd never been there.

*

Brad's salmon-brick house in Nollamara was the same. No Charger parked out front. The screen door locked. No signs of life inside. No cereal packets on the benches or dishes in the sink. No television on the milk crate in the corner of the lounge, or sheets on the bed. Lee walked down the drive and peered over the fence. No tools scattered about or clothes on the Hills hoist. Even the garden hose was gone from the driveway tap that dripped into the grey earth.

23.

The Royal Perth Hospital waiting room was crowded. In the first row of chairs a grey-haired Aboriginal couple leaned into one another. The man was wrapped in a red blanket and the old woman cradled a baby that wouldn't stop crying. A white teenager with red eyes sat beside his mother. The laces on his football boots were undone and mud from the boot-sprigs was crumbled in a halo around his feet. A skinny man with a sunburned face leaned forward, spitting into a cup, wheezing and coughing, a blue tint on his lips. Dozens of patients behind them, all the seats taken.

Lee asked the duty nurse if he could see his father. She didn't know the name and looked down her clipboard and made a call. He saw the change of expression come into her eyes, and then the glance at his jeans, his workboots, pretending that she was looking past him. She put down the phone and took a breath. 'Can I have a name, please? Mr Southern is still recovering from being operated on. He isn't conscious yet, but if you want to take a seat, and wait...'

Lee caught the tone in her voice.

'No thanks. I'll come back in a couple of hours.'

The Ford was parked on a sloping lot in the shadow of the Catholic cathedral across the road. Lee unlocked the steel tray-box and took out the blue scrubs that he'd taken from Frankie's room. They were tucked away in a bottom drawer; likely from someone she'd brought home. They weren't washed, and had yellow stains on the front legs. Smelled gastric.

Lee slipped the trousers over his jeans. Took off his t-shirt and put on the sleeveless top, smoothed it over the Luger at his waist.

*

At the service entrance he took a wheelchair and kicked off the brake and pushed it through the heavy striped doors that were marked with black boot-prints. He walked to the nearest lift and pressed floor number two. He didn't know where he was going. The corridors of the second floor were busy with emergency staff going about their business. Men pushing trolleys laden with soiled sheets. They wore white uniforms. He saw a young doctor shining a light into the eyes of a child with a bleeding head, wearing the same blue scrubs that Lee wore. Theatre nurses in Frankie's green scrubs and ward nurses wearing the white aprons gathered around. Two orderlies in white uniforms transferred a groaning old woman from an ambulance trolley to a hospital bed. Older nurses in little ward stations separated by low glass walls.

All the doctors and nurses wore ID tags and different lanyards, but not the orderlies.

Lee wasn't going to pass for a doctor.

He found a bank of desks that were covered with clipboards and files of different colours. He took one of the files and entered the room behind the desks. It was a linen room where staff also kept their valuables. He didn't touch the handbags and shoulder bags but took up a pile of white folded uniforms like the orderlies wore, and felt his way through the collars until he found his size. He locked the door and took off the doctor's scrubs and dressed himself like an orderly. Stowed the soiled doctor's scrubs behind a pile of white sheets. Exchanged the wheelchair out in the triage room for a trolley containing toiletry materials – paper towels, liquid soap, fresh bedpans and adult nappies.

Lee got out of the lift at the highest floor. He didn't know where the operation had taken place. He only knew that his father was still a prisoner, and that he'd be under guard. It made sense that he'd be kept on the higher floors.

This floor was made up of wards and private rooms. Through the windows in the various wards he could see the city skyline and the river to the south, the tops of giant eucalypts swaying in the sea breeze. He pushed the trolley around the different rooms, keeping his eyes down when he passed a nurse or a doctor. The rooms smelled of disinfectant and fresh laundry. Within the wards, most of the beds were curtained, and he had to stop and peer into each one. It was while opening another curtain to reveal a sleeping young woman with her hands clasped around a teddy bear that he heard the voice.

The old man's voice – coming from the television bolted to the ceiling. Lee parked his trolley in the hall and sat on the chair beside the sleeping woman.

There was no doubt about it.

It was the old man – Kinslow's superior – the leader of the APM. The same accent and intonation.

A strap of text at the bottom of the screen read *General Brian Paxton*.

Now there was a face to go with the voice. Lee listened to the words but was captivated by the man's dark eyes, his imperious hand gestures, his angled head when he thought a question unworthy.

He was being interviewed because it'd been leaked that General Paxton was about to be announced by the Premier as the new Governor of the State of Western Australia, subject to the Queen's approval. A man with a long and distinguished military career. Started out as a ranking commando officer in WW2, was there at the St Nazaire Raid where he won a Victoria Cross. Had migrated to Australia in the early 1950s, became a lawyer but then joined the Australian Regular Army as a second lieutenant to fight in Korea, then saw service with the SAS in Malaya, Borneo, and finally Vietnam.

'I'm flattered by your questions, but I am not able to confirm or deny this rumour. Saying that, I have dedicated my life to the service of this nation, and I couldn't think of a higher honour. Thank you.'

With that, Paxton turned on his heels and went up the

veranda stairs and into the dark house, the cameras still rolling. Lee could smell the jasmine flowers that clumped over the veranda railings, because he'd been there, and smelled them. Could remember the sound of boots on the bare boards, the wiping of feet on the doormat, the smell of polished wood and Brasso inside the house until he was dragged down into the limestone cellar.

The vision was cut, and the television news segued to coverage of the right-wing rally outside Parliament House, a sea of Australian and Southern Cross flags, Kinslow addressing the assembled skinheads and others wearing the Celtic cross on t-shirts and peaked caps. Not a Nazi flag to be seen, just a banner reading *Australian Patriotic Movement*. Men and women, young and old. A few children, the wind-buffeted voice of Kinslow, speaking through a megaphone: '… Even our federal parliamentarians have seen reason and made their voices known, as we all must do at the coming election.'

Someone passed outside the curtain, humming a Neil Diamond tune. Lee waited until they'd gone and took his trolley, the front left wheel squeaking on the linoleum floor. There were a few private rooms toward the end of the hall, two of them dark and three of them lit up. The darkened rooms contained a sleeping shape that was too large to be his father. A sad whistling snore emanated from an old woman in the next room. Lee bypassed the next two rooms and arrived at the corner room whose curtains were pulled and door shut. There was no scrawled patient name tag on this door, unlike the others. He listened for a while, and then turned the doorknob. He saw the copper's polished boots this side of the bed. There was an ensuite shower and toilet to the side, and Lee wheeled in the trolley and parked it against the wall. The young constable looked at him and shrugged, made exasperated eyes. He was tall and thin and had a pronounced Adam's apple and a long nose. He glanced at his watch and shook his head.

'I'm gonna be here a minute, cleaning up, if you want a break.'

The constable looked wary, but when Lee began unpacking some paper towels and took up a large bottle of pink liquid soap, clearly not caring either way, he scratched his nose and looked at his watch again. Lee followed him in the reflection off the bathroom mirror through the open door.

'I might do that. Thanks. Got another six hours of this and I've gone through the gossip mags already. Whaddo I care if Kylie and Craig are getting it off? Hard to tell 'em apart, with that poodle hair.'

'No worries. Like I say, I'm gonna be here.'

The copper took a packet of Winfield Blues from his shirt pocket and tapped one out, shuffled toward the door.

Lee had avoided looking at his father and he was glad of it. The sight of him so small and thin, his bony shoulders above the bandages that wrapped his chest, would have given him away.

His eyes were shut, and air snickered through his nose. His long hair was sweat-plastered on his forehead, despite the chill in the room. His lips were grey and his sunken eye sockets caught shadow.

At least he wasn't handcuffed to the bed. No need for that, just yet.

Lee sat in the copper's seat, dragged himself alongside the bed, took his father's hand in his own.

He looked at each of the tattoos that were so familiar. The wedge-tailed eagle, coming in to land on his chest with its talons out, smudged now with age. The equally smudged dagger and motto of the SAS, on his forearm. Lee's solid black handprint on the ball of his shoulder, which he'd done when Lee was seven. His father had made Lee photocopy his hand in the council library and then took him to the backyard bikie tattooist in Dongara, whose homemade gun drilled away on its buzzing elastic band while he wiped the irritated skin with a green and white dishrag. The pair of them talked about bikes and American bands while Lee pretended to read from the latest *Commando* comic that he bought weekly from the newsagent. Every now and then the tattooist would shake the hair from his sweaty face and look at Lee and shout 'Donner und Blitzen!' or 'Gott im Himmel' or 'Raus, raus, raus!' then crack up laughing.

His father moaned softly now, and his lips moved, his tongue searching for moisture inside his open mouth, making a shucking sound.

Lee squeezed his father's hand, and whispered, 'I'm here,' but his father's eyes never opened. He had always been wiry and lean, the product of hard work, a starvation diet and too much speed, but now the muscles in his arms were pliant and soft.

Lee heard the squeak of two sets of shoes in the hallway, and he replaced his father's hand on the bed, but he didn't move the chair back to its position.

When the copper returned he was going to lie, and say that the man had woken, had asked him to sit there for a while, to not leave him.

But it wasn't the copper.

Lee saw her profile through the glass and the face of the man beside. It was Robbie, Kinslow's boy, with Frankie.

They rolled into the room, both of them registering surprise when they saw him. Frankie's mouth made a snarl, and Robbie, wearing the same white orderly's uniform as Lee, reached behind his back and drew out the cattle prod.

Frankie was carrying a tray. On the tray was a syringe, and a swab.

Lee stood to protect his father.

Frankie had access to all kinds of medicine, but she'd chosen Drano to put into Lee's arm. She'd wanted him to suffer as he died.

'Paxton's your father, isn't he? The old man.'

She didn't answer. Very carefully, she picked up the syringe, tossed the tray onto the bed, held the syringe underhand like a knife. Lee could see the training in her movements.

But Robbie put his hand in front of her, stepped forward, smiling perversely, waving the crackling prod.

Lee had his Luger, but remembered his father's words, to

never draw a weapon unless you were prepared to use it.

Gunshots in the hospital – he didn't want that.

They both came at him.

Lee got inside the prod and watched the needle catch in his shirt, the world slowing down as Lee's hand on Robbie's forearm brought the prod onto Frankie's shoulder. He heard her cry out, her right arm gone dead, her limp fingers a frozen point in the blur of hands as she took the syringe into her left hand and thrust it toward him. Lee dropped a knee and took Robbie's weight, threw him onto the syringe.

Frankie stood back. Robbie didn't feel it at first. Struggled with Lee's hand at his throat, fingers closing on the carotids while his knee sank itself home. He felt Robbie begin to close down. The tension left his body. Frankie backed out of the room, cradling her deadened arm. Lee watched the lights go out in Robbie's eyes, surprise and then fear as one eye drooped shut, while in the open eye blood vessels began to burst like fireworks, and then he was on the floor.

Lee stood and straightened his shirt. Dragged Robbie into the bathroom and pushed in the trolley and shut the door. He looked down at his father, unconscious still. There was a cannula in his left forearm connected to a drip. Lee pulled it out of his arm, put a blanket over him to hide the bleeding. Kicked at each of the wheel brakes and shoved the bed around the room and into the hall.

The lift was down the other end of the corridor. He didn't know where Frankie had gone. Any moment he expected the lift to open and the copper to emerge, but it didn't happen like that. Lee elbowed the button and waited, and when the empty lift arrived he pushed the bed inside and pressed for the ground floor, watching his father's gaunt face all the way down.

The lift doors opened and he scanned the busy emergency floor. The only exits were the patient doors to the waiting room and the double doors to the ambulance ramp. He skirted the beds and chairs in their block formations where men and women in various states of distress were looked after by kneeling doctors and teams of nurses. He hit the red button to open the ambulance doors and the hiss was loud and made him flinch.

He told himself to breathe, wheeling the bed past two parked ambulances whose drivers sat and watched him pass and an empty ambulance at the rear whose driver was chatting to one of the others. Lee cut behind the final ambulance so that he'd be out of sight and walked backwards down the ramp past the low hedges and concrete barriers until he was on the street. It was only when he turned the corner that he saw the coppers at his tow truck. One TRG van and three police sedans, lights flashing but sirens off. Lee turned the bed around and kept his shoulders low and went back up the ramp. His father was murmuring now, smacking his lips, clenching his fingers and toes, a sign that he was coming out into pain.

The first ambulance in the line had gone and the second ambulance was empty. Lee opened the rear doors of the third ambulance and locked the wheels of the bed and looked down at his father.

The only way he knew how to support another man's weight was the fireman's carry, but he didn't want to open his father's chest wound. He looked at the folded ambulance bed in its grooves, and unlocked its rear brakes and pulled it out the back. It unfolded as it emerged. Lee kicked on the brakes. He got behind his father and took him under the armpits and shuffled him over, his father's eyes opening for a moment and looking at him. Lee swung his father's legs over and didn't know what to do next. He took a risk and slammed the folding bed against the rear of the ambulance and it folded automatically and he pushed and hoisted it until the wheels were locked in their grooves. Lee slammed the doors shut and went and climbed in the driver's side.

The keys were in the ignition.

He put it into drive, pulled out behind the parked ambulance and drove down the ramp. He reached the street, the right lane protected by a concrete barrier. There was an ambulance cap on the seat beside, and he put it on. He had no choice but to drive past his tow truck where coppers were digging around inside the cab and prying open his tray-box while the darkly clad TRG stood around and watched. Lee ducked his head as he approached, and picked up the short-wave radio mike on the dash and pretended to speak into it. One of the tallest TRG officers, toting a pump-action shotgun, unstrapped his black helmet and slid it from his head.

It was Brad, wiping sweat from his eyes with the back of his hand, looking around the streets for Lee.

The TRG didn't capture fugitives. They were called in when

suspects were armed, as Lee was armed. They shot them down.

Lee could hear Frankie's voice in his head. 'This is why we don't isolate ourselves from the institutions of government. This is why we infiltrate state power and turn it to our own ends.'

Brad lit a cigarette as Lee approached, the officer turning to look at the ambulance, Lee tilting his palm in a gesture of greeting.

One state servant waving to another.

Brad ignored him and spat at his feet.

24.

The freeway was jammed with late-afternoon commuters, but Lee figured how to work the flashing lights and drove the emergency lane, headed south. The sun was moving to the horizon across the golden river. He didn't know what to do next, except that as soon as the ambulance was reported missing, those coppers at the scene would put his father's disappearance together with the stolen vehicle and then every copper in the city would be looking for them, including the TRG.

Lee exited the freeway at Canning Bridge and headed toward Fremantle. It was nearly six o'clock and he remembered the hire-car depot next to the boxing gym on South Street. He cut the flashing lights and took suburban backstreets until he reached the industrial area beside the cemetery, and knew that he was close.

The lights were out in the depot office and the length of chain that crossed the entrance was low to the ground. There was traffic behind him but no pedestrians on the street. He drove the ambulance slowly forward, catching the heavy chain on the front bumper. He revved and pushed, felt the chain resist and the engine whine, and then the chain snapped at the lock.

He drove into the depot and parked under the carwash. Opened the back doors of the ambulance and looked for something resembling a slim jim. He found a steel tongue depressor in a set of drawers and crawled backwards but something grabbed his arm. He flinched, but looked down into his father's eyes.

'Son, I wanted you to leave. I want you to leave.'

There was no time to explain. Lee only said, 'They tried to kill you, at the hospital. Same way they tried to get rid of me.'

That was enough for his father, who pursed his lips and nodded, closed his eyes.

Lee sidled up to a Budget transit van, looked up the street again and slid in the tongue depressor and heard the lock click open. He turned, and there was Gerry, the old boxer, carrying his gloves, a towel around his neck.

Lee ignored the man's stare. Got inside the van and ripped off the plastic cowling under the steering wheel, went to work with his trembling fingers and teeth, stripping back the plastic sheathing. Joined the wires and heard the engine kick. Worked the copper wires together to form a twist and backed across the depot to the rear door of the ambulance.

Gerry stood at the rear doors, glancing at Lee's father.

Lee nodded to him but his voice was hard. 'You don't

wanna get involved here, Mr Tracker.'

'Too late for that. It's all over the radio.'

Three teenage Noongar boys that Lee recognised from the gym cut across the depot carpark and stood behind them, watching. Gerry hoisted a thumb in the direction of the gym. 'Come on, get movin. Nothin to see here. I'll be down in a minute.'

Gerry dropped his gloves and took one side of the ambulance bed and Lee took the other. Together, they carried the bed across to the transit van, without dropping the legs.

Lee shut the rear doors.

'You got money?' Gerry asked.

'Yeah, I got money.'

'You got medicine? He's gonna need it.'

Lee shook his head and they climbed into the ambulance and began emptying the coloured plastic drawers in the side walls onto a blanket between them. Lee balled the pile of syringes and bandages and ampoules up in his fist and they got out together.

'Get goin. I'll park the meat wagon round the back. Won't be found until tomorrow.'

Lee put out his hand, and the other man shook it, then moved away. Lee got in the van and put it in gear. As he pulled to the road and indicated left, he watched Gerry climb into the ambulance and drive it round the corner and out of sight.

*

They spent the night parked in another rental car depot in Welshpool, surrounded by factories, trucking stations and abandoned silos. Lee put up the blanket to separate the cab from the rear bay. He held up each of the ampoules to the streetlight and tried to work out what was useful. His father drifted in and out of consciousness and each time he awoke he tried to get up and Lee held him down. Just before dawn he awoke and his eyes were clear with pain. Lee was ready with a syringe full of pethidine which he injected into his father's thigh. He watched the relief come over his father's face, although this time he stayed awake, insisted on holding Lee's forearm, squeezing as he squeezed out the words.

'I got a mate. He's a medic from Nam. Lives in the hills over there in Jarrahdale. He'll take me in.'

'Dad, we got to run. Far away as possible.'

Lee's father smiled weakly. 'That's what they're expectin. All this shit about the dead Governor, they'll be checkin roads out of Perth. Better to hide in plain sight. Then *you* run.'

Lee shook his head. He didn't want to tell his father about the Governor, not yet. 'We run, together.'

The laugh that his father attempted got strangled in a gurgling wheeze. 'Damn bullet tore through one of my lungs. Went straight out the back. But no, son. I'm gonna talk now, and you're gonna listen.'

Jack Southern paused, caught the look on Lee's face.

'What is it?' he asked.

Lee looked away, looked back. 'Nothing. Kinslow tried to get into my head, told me some things.'

Now it was Jack Southern's turn to look away. He wiped a hand over his eyes, notched his brow. 'Well, you said it. Tried to get into your head. Why I protected you from those people. Kinslow's always been a snake. Always had ambitions. Not surprising he's gone into politics. You can't believe a word that –'

'Dad ... stop.'

Lee's father did as he was told. Closed his eyes, then opened them again. Opened his mouth to speak, but thought better of it. Gave Lee a weak nod.

'What Kinslow told me about you in Vietnam. It's true, isn't it? You took a scalpel to yourself. You were sick. They sent you home.'

Jack Southern was silent for a long while, staring back at Lee, hurt in his eyes.

'Why didn't you tell me?' Lee asked. 'What else didn't you tell me?'

'Ok ... Enough.' Jack Southern's voice dropped to a whisper. It wasn't clear whether he was speaking to himself, or to Lee, who leaned in.

'Son, you've been loyal to me, but I've been bad for you. Locked up these past months, I had to straighten my head.'

'You're bleedin again.'

It was true. A bloom of fresh blood was spreading out from the rust circle of dried blood at his father's breast, looked like a flower opening its petals.

'Listen to what I'm sayin.'

'I am. I want to know.'

'You're a good son, and you're gonna make a fine man. But

I've never been straight with you. Now you're ready to know the truth, and that's good. Some things I got to tell you, in case things don't work out for me. First, is that I know where your mother is. You go to her – she'll take you in. She never did run off and abandon you, like I said. I *made* her leave. She didn't like the way things was headed, the way I was when I got back from Nam. I put a gun to her head and made her leave, son, told her never to return or make contact again, or I'd hunt her down. I wanted you for myself. I wanted to make you safe from what's comin. I wanted to make you into what I wanted to make myself. And I *did.*'

Lee tried to take back his arm, but his father gripped with a surprising strength.

'I don't blame you, son. You're gonna hate me for that, and more. That's on me.'

Lee had kept himself awake through the night, despite the fatigue, the adrenalin leaking out and weighing him down. Now he felt the familiar surge of anger that his father had taught him to turn into clarity and action.

But behind it was something else, unexpected, the return of a feeling that he'd long thought abandoned, and it felt like sadness and it spoke in his mother's voice.

'What else? What else you got to tell me?'

His father closed his eyes and nodded, the spitefulness in Lee's voice some kind of reassurance to him. 'You got Abo blood, Lee. My grandma. Our camp off the Thundellara Track? We got roots there goin right back beyond my grandpa Donal Southern.'

Lee didn't know what to say. Everything his father was telling him was a surprise, and not a surprise. 'Why didn't you tell me?'

'Same reason my dad didn't tell me. Your great-grandpa Donal took your grandpa Vernon into town. They never spoke about it. Vernon was pale-skinned and he could pass as a white. There was nothin good in them days bein an Abo, and if Donal wanted to keep his son, he had to say that Vernon was white. Donal's black wife had died so there was no proof it was any different. It was your mother who asked Vernon one day, and he told her straight up. *I* didn't know. That's how *I* found out. It was part of the problems between us, in the end. Part of me wanting her away from you.'

Lee spoke through gritted teeth. 'Anythin else? Is there anything else? What about Vietnam? The Knights?'

His father's breathing was settling, his fingers went limp on Lee's arm. 'Another time, Lee. There's nothing else I want to say now, except that I'm sorry. Get me a pen. You've got to write those addresses.'

Lee took down the addresses of the medic and his mother and sat beside his father, watching his chest rise and fall, listening to the freight traffic on the highway as the light came over the hills.

Lee climbed into the driver's seat and drew up a syringe-full of pethidine and stabbed it in his thigh, felt the warmth flush through him, much like the sunlight now filling out the darkness in the parking lot, sketching details into the shadow.

He looked at his watch, and connected the ignition wires.

Flicked through the UBD until he found the right map. Pulled out of the parking lot and turned toward the hills.

*

The medic lived on a north-facing hillside behind a stand of she-oak, the wind whispering through the green needles in the higher branches as Lee guided the van up the hill. The dirt track was guttered and potholed, the red earth edged with dried streams. Like most of his father's Vietnam mates, the medic lived at the end of a long drive, wanted to hear the sound of anyone coming to meet him.

It took Lee three minutes to reach the rammed-earth house, built into the hillside, the tin roof catching the morning glare. A low stone wall circled the house like a rampart. Three kangaroo dogs strained at their ropes beside the garage.

Lee saw movement behind the tinted window at the front door. He backed up the van to the house and climbed out, his hands in the air.

He knew the drill.

The medic cracked the flyscreen, a short man whose eyes glinted behind a mop of grey hair.

'I'm Lee Southern. I got my father here, who needs some attention.'

The medic looked past Lee's shoulder, down the track.

'Don't worry, I wasn't followed. The van is fresh stolen.'

The medic left the doorway, leaning something behind the jamb. He wore tracksuit pants and ugg boots with gaffer tape on the toes, a faded blue singlet.

'I been expecting you since I saw the news. I got everything ready inside.'

Lee opened the van's rear doors and they carried out the trolley, kicked down the legs, wheeled it along a corridor into a spare room with a tiled floor and walls. A laundry basin and a hose. A drain in the corner.

Nothing else except a refrigerator and a kerosene heater that the medic turned to maximum.

Lee returned with the blanket full of medicine, laid it on the floor next to the trolley-bed. The medic glanced at it and nodded. 'I got everything we need here, sonny. From those pinhole eyes of yours, I reckon you'd best take some of that for yourself.'

Lee picked up a handful of the glass ampoules and pill bottles and put them in his hat, followed the medic out the front door. The medic walked down the side of the van and went into his garage and came back with a Stanley knife.

'You start peeling off those decals. I'll be back in a sec.'

Lee did as he was told, peeling off the foot-high Budget Rent a Car decals on the sides of the van, the stickers on the rear window. The medic returned with two number plates and an unopened envelope.

'Peel off the rego on the front window, replace it with this. These plates and rego match.'

The medic knelt and began unscrewing the licence plates while Lee peeled off the rego from the front windscreen, replacing it with the brand new registration in the envelope. According to the licence papers, the rego belonged to a Mr

Terrence Daly who resided at the medic's address, and was made out for an '83 Holden Commodore.

The medic stood with the stolen plates and tossed the screwdriver in his hand, looking over his work. 'Unless you're caught speeding or make a copper suspicious at a roadblock, this'll pass muster. Those plates and rego are legit, for just this purpose.'

Lee passed the medic a cigarette, but he shook his head. 'Son, I'm operatin on one lung, a quarter of my liver and a shitload of pills.'

Back in the tiled room, his father was awake, sweat beaded on his forehead. The medic wheeled in a drip stand. He opened the fridge door and took out a bag of saline solution. Went and pressed his thumbs into Lee's father's wrist where the cannula had been taken out. 'Good to see you again, old mate. Blood type O, isn't it?'

'Yeah, it is.'

'Got plenty of that in the freezer, if we need it. Now let me have a look at that wound, front and back. You sit up?'

Jack Southern nodded, but put up a hand, called Lee over. 'You go and see her now. Like I said, she'll take you in.'

'Nah. I'll come back for you in a couple of weeks, when you're healed up. We'll go to the camps north, live up there for a while.'

Lee's father shook his head. 'Soon as I'm healed enough to be able to defend myself, I'm handin myself in. I can do that time, and I've got mates inside. That's the smart play here. You be smart too. Go and see her. Then head east. Write to me after a year, when the heat's off.'

Lee bent and embraced his father, who winced. Lee looked into his father's eyes. It had been dark in the van last night, and he hadn't seen it. The new clarity there, as though his father had given something up.

He looked at peace, for the first time Lee could remember.

25.

Lee drove east on Jarrahdale Road toward Albany Highway when the clock ticked over the hour and the news came on the radio. He expected the lead news to be about his father going missing, or the murder of the Governor, and he was braced for talk of sightings of his father or of roadblocks and raids, but the newsreader led with a breaking story about a young woman's kidnapping from a public street. The next words hit him hard: '… taken from outside an exclusive girls school in broad daylight this morning, as she got out of a bus … Three men in balaclavas. Speeding away in a white van. Police calling for members of the public …'

Lee realised he was climbing in third, the van close to stalling. A horn blast from behind. He pulled into a bus stop and killed the engine. Fumbled for a cigarette. Punched the dash until his knuckles were bloody.

*

Lee parked the van on the South Perth foreshore, looked

across at the city, so quiet and still in the morning light. The traffic on the bridge and the freeway interchanges distant enough to be nothing more than a background rumble. He smoked cigarette after cigarette until the early afternoon, then gave himself another shot in the thigh.

It was all because of that stupid letter. His foolish dream that a girl like Emma and a boy like him could be together, in the face of everything that said otherwise.

All he'd done was put her in danger.

There was nobody he could go to. There was nothing to say. Who would believe him?

Lee thought instead about Frankie and the old man, Paxton, her father. Brad and Kinslow. Robbie and the others. Concentrated all of his hatred on them.

They had kidnapped Emma because they knew that Lee would come for her, and then they would kill him.

*

The sun was setting over the dark river, glistening like snakeskin. Lee circled the riverside parade looking for somewhere to park, the white mansion walls glowing even as the lush vegetation behind the walls began to disappear into shadow. There wasn't anybody on the street. The only signs of life were at the local tennis and bowling clubs. He thought about parking on the Point Resolution bluff, but the carpark was empty, and the police were looking for a white van that had taken Emma. He chose the bowling club, where old men in creams rolled balls across the minty grass, then he drove back to the nearest shopping centre. He bought two large steaks and found a public phone outside a small cinema.

Lee dropped the coin and dialled the number that'd been played over and over on the radio. He didn't bother shielding his voice. He only spoke for a few seconds, giving the address where he knew Emma was being kept.

Lee dropped another coin and this time dialled the operator. When he got the number he wanted, he made the call. He could hear the sound of leather hitting leather, the grunts and slaps of the gym. When Gerry came on the phone, Lee spoke. 'You knew, didn't you? Soon as you saw me, you knew.'

The older man didn't speak for a while. When he did, his voice was gentle. 'Sure I did. But knowing and saying, they don't always go together. There's lots of people I see like you, but that doesn't mean they're ready, or willin to hear. You there, son?'

'I'm here.'

'I'm a Yamatji man myself. Sure as shit, my mob bein from up there, I'll know how to connect you in. When you ready. You know where to find me.'

'Thanks. I will. I appreciate that.'

*

At the bowling club, Lee parked against a yellow skip bin with a view of the mansion across the street. He cleaned the Luger and replaced each of the seven bullets in the magazine, making sure there was one in the breech. After half an hour he gave himself another shot in the thigh, then swallowed two brown bombers to keep himself awake and sharpen his nerves. He lit a cigarette and sat back to wait.

It was another hour before the police wagon arrived. Two uniformed police got out, and Lee could tell from the tentative way they carried themselves how it was going to go. The pair walked down the sloping driveway and disappeared from view. It was only a minute before they returned, got back in the wagon and drove away.

Lee thought about how to breach the mansion walls. When Brad had murdered the Governor, they'd crossed several backyards to get to the private residence, and he'd be expecting Lee to do the same. Lee had already scoped what lay at the end of the driveway, when he'd followed Frankie and caught a glimpse of General Paxton, not knowing then who he was. A high steel gate, with intercom and security cameras. Two Doberman guard dogs. No doubt an APM heavy stationed there too.

Lee took a swig from his water bottle and climbed out of the van. He stowed the Luger in his belt and took the steaks wrapped in butcher's paper. He'd studded them with crushed Rohypnol tablets taken from the ambulance.

Lee walked along the road that led to Point Resolution, then took small paths through the weedy scrub until he reached the river. The tide was up and he could see the phosphorescent churn of current in the dark water. Limestone rocks and small reefs broke the shore, algae, sea lettuce and brown and white jellyfish washed to the tideline. Up ahead, a large water rat swam in the shallows and scampered away when he approached, disappearing into a clump of sedge-grass.

Lee counted the houses as he stepped over the reef. Above him, behind the high walls, he heard the tinkle of a piano and smelled barbequed meat, freshly watered grass and chlorinated swimming pools.

Paxton's mansion was built onto a cliff that rose over the river and was too steep to climb. Lee clambered up to the limestone wall of the mansion beside, and edged himself along until he was at the base of Paxton's wall. The painted breezeblock was ten foot high and devoid of fingerholds. At the top of the wall Lee could see the glinting of broken bottles cemented along the crest, illuminated by the moon. He wedged himself into the corner between the two walls. The foot-length space was rough and grippy, enabling him to chimney-climb until he was able to reach the crest of the neighbour's wall. He lay on the top of the wall and looked into the rear of the house that was dark and quiet. The patio furniture was covered in canvas tarpaulin, and there were no lights behind the tinted glass. Paxton's wall was another three feet higher, and Lee crouched and peered into the old man's sprawling and sloping yard, built like an Italian grotto with raised limestone garden beds and rough limestone arches that looked like the entrances to caves. A couple of olive trees and grapevines on a trellis overhanging the rear patio. The house blazing with light. Two storeys, and every room with curtains open.

He had cover where he was crouched. Clumps of banana and palm tree pushed above the neighbour's wall, shielding him from any view down the line.

There was no need to hurry.

They were expecting him, after all.

The appearance of the police would have confirmed this, as he'd planned.

But whatever happened next, he wanted the police to have a record of their visit, and his call.

A few minutes later Lee saw a dark shape emerge from the side of the house, and he ducked beneath the parapet wall. He heard boot-steps on limestone rubble, and then the eager panting of the dogs.

Lee waited until the guard was gone, then returned to his surveillance. The dogs were on the back porch, playing tug of war with a rope. Lee unfolded the steaks and leaned over and dropped them both, feet apart, onto the path.

He waited for the dogs to bark, but there was nothing. He could hear them snuffling closer, and the wet chomping of their jaws at work.

Lee waited until they'd left before he stole a glance over the fence. The dogs were back at play on the porch, lanky shadows silhouetted against the bright light of the kitchen behind them.

He watched and waited for them to tire. One of them whined and sat, wiping its paws over its face. The other dropped the rope and went and licked the other's face. It too sat, and laid its chin over the other dog's back, then closed its eyes.

When he was sure that they were both asleep, Lee crawled onto the parapet wall and dropped the ten feet onto the gravel.

The sound was louder than he expected, and he felt a spike of adrenalin rise from his guts and spread to his shaking hands. He took out his Luger and switched off the safety and scurried to the side of the house. He glanced inside the patio doors, but couldn't see anyone. He moved to the edge of the patio and waited for the guard's shadow to appear. He kept his back against the wall, and his ears alert to the sound of windows opening or door-locks behind him.

Lee used the time to steady his breathing, loading his blood with oxygen, hoping to clear his mind of the chemicals of fear. But despite his training, his heartbeat was rising, and his palm was clammy on the crosshatched grip of the pistol. He felt the need to move, to burn off the tense energy that was pumping through his body, making him feel light-headed and weak.

Lee was better trained than most soldiers in the ADF, but this wasn't training.

He listened to his father's voice, telling him to breathe. He held the breath for a few seconds until he released and sucked in another lungful, allowing his belly to breathe for him, waiting for the shadow on the wall.

When it came, a long angled shadow accompanied by the crunching of boots on gravel, Lee was nearly overcome with panic, and overcompensated by striking out early, the butt of his Luger catching the man's face rather than the side of his head. The guard cried out, automatically reaching for his crushed nose. Lee kicked out from the porch and caught the man in the midriff, winding him and doubling him over. The guard righted himself by reaching for Lee's legs, knocking him off balance. Lee went with it and rolled into the pathway, keeping himself above the guard who he struck with an elbow and then another. There was a sharp pain in Lee's side and he knew that he'd been stabbed in the hip and he rose above and tried to get at the guard's arms but then he heard a low growling and saw the dark shape on the edges of his vision. He pushed himself toward the wall and let the guard raise himself and now Lee was prone and the Doberman fixed its jaws around the man's shoulder while Lee got out from under him. The dog was still dazed and didn't notice him crawl away. Only one of the dogs had woken and Lee got onto his feet and backed to the wall. The man was shouting as the dog now tugged at his hands. The dog's movements weren't coordinated, and its legs kept buckling, but the distraction allowed Lee to get behind the man and launch a kick into the back of his head. The sound was ugly and the dog fell sideways, crawling on its paws beside the unconscious man, looking up at Lee and the pistol in his hand. It closed its eyes and he stepped around it, continued in the direction the guard had come from.

The front yard was brightly lit. Lee climbed onto the balcony that he knew from the television interview wrapped the front of the house. Bamboo furniture and a barbeque and potted plants. He could smell the jasmine as he edged across to each window and peered inside. There was nobody visible, and the only sound was some frogs in a nearby pond and the strumming of cicadas and laughter from over at the bowling club.

There was nobody by the front door, which was open. It

smelled of a trap, but there was nothing for it. Lee went in low and quiet.

He moved through the house, looking for the cellar. The same smell of polished wood and Brasso. Photographs of Paxton and Frankie, on holidays in Europe, by the Pisa and Eiffel towers, on a gondola in Venice. Paxton in three sets of uniforms within the same picture frame. Young and handsome, wearing the British para beret, then later in SAS baggy greens and another in full dress uniform, receiving a medal from Her Majesty.

The door to the cellar was in the laundry, and it was open. He could smell the rough limestone walls, musty and dry, as he aimed his pistol down the stairs. It was semi-dark, lit by a dull globe. All he could see was a wall of bottles. Wine bottles, layered with dust, necks facing out. Shelves laden with whisky and clear spirits in pretty bottles.

'Come down, young man. We've been waiting for you.'

Paxton's voice was mildly amused. 'And come down without your weapon, or your friend will suffer the consequences.'

'Hurry up, Lee. Let's get this over with.' Frankie, sounding bored.

Lee looked around for something to roll down the stairs, anything to create a diversion and break up the static pattern of bodies waiting for him.

'We're waiting,' Frankie said. 'Actually, you know what? I think we need to hurt her some more.'

There was nothing to hand. Just some powdered bleach and bars of soap. Shoe polish. A bottle of methylated spirits.

Given time, he could make something of that, but …

Lee heard the unmistakable sound of a cattle prod crackling to life. He imagined Emma's face.

'Throw your Luger to the foot of the stairs,' Paxton said, 'or your friend will be hurt.'

'Ok. I'm coming down.'

'Good boy. Place your hands on the railings as you descend. You move, she dies. There's no need for you both to suffer.'

It was those last words from Paxton. The certainty behind the smugness.

Once they killed Lee, there was no chance that they'd let Emma live.

'You let me see her, and I'll come down.'

'Throw the Luger. Last chance.'

Lee tossed the Luger down the stairs. It landed on the bottom step and slid onto the cement floor.

He grabbed a singlet from the clothes basket at his feet. Twisted off the cap from the metho bottle, thrust half the rolled singlet inside, tilted it up. When the rag was stained wet he lit it with his lighter, watched the blue flames and black smoke turn over his hand.

He reached for the heavy iron doorstop, shaped into the form of a Balinese dragon.

'You know she's here. There's no need to see her.'

Lee stood in the doorway and aimed with the doorstop. Threw it hard into the shelves of spirits and released the Molotov as he dive-rolled down the stairs, scrabbling for the Luger and hitting the cement while above him the wall exploded as the gases in the metho and the shattered spirits met the flame, a searing shockwave that filled the room and blasted over him. Bullets smacked behind him, dust from the walls and roiling black smoke filling the room. He lay on his belly and saw Brad firing into the smoke, fired the Luger into his guts, his chest. Frankie was standing next to her father, a look of black shock on her face, a jagged splinter of glass caught in her throat, the cattle prod hanging in her hands. Only Paxton was calm, holding the hooded Emma by the neck and forehead, ready to twist and snap. She was limp in the chair, her hands lolling.

Paxton was unarmed.

Behind him, wine bottles cracked in the heat, dozens of bottles, then hundreds, a cascade of ruby red wine filtering through the shattering glass, a tinkling, musical sound as it fell through the racks.

The flames were lapping up and eating the floorboards, curling over their heads. Lee had two bullets left. Paxton firmed his grip on Emma's head and made ready to break her neck.

Beside him, Frankie fell to her knees, and then Paxton saw the jagged shard in her neck, leaking arterial blood, and he shouted, and Lee took the shots, two in quick succession, saw the blush of red mist and shattered teeth emerge from Paxton's mouth, then the pop beneath his right eyeball, instantly bloody, pooling in the reddening light, both his hands rising as he fell backwards into the flames.

Emma was still limp in her chair, a puddle of urine beneath

her. He picked her up in a fireman's carry and made for the stairs.

He didn't take off the hood as he placed her onto the kitchen bench. He went to the stove and turned on the gas elements, went to the rear of the house and opened every window, every door.

The old house was screaming, sighing. Flames spurted across wood-panelled walls and onto curtains and blinds. Rising up the stairwell bannisters, eating the varnish and wooden steps.

On the back patio, the dogs were looking into the house, unsteady on their feet and edging away, out into the darkness.

Lee made for the front door, pressed to open the gate. He staggered up the driveway and crossed the street and bowling club carpark and opened the van door. He placed Emma onto the passenger seat. He ran around the car and started it up, backed across the lot.

Nobody inside the club had noticed the golden glow and the crackling trees down by the river. Lee turned onto Riverside Drive and pulled off Emma's hood and looked into her eyes, then tore out the gag in her mouth. She began to spit and wheeze and offered up her bound hands, and he steered and undid the binds.

Lee wound down the window and headed for the coast, neither of them talking, Emma sobbing and then the shaking began in Lee's hands as he realised that he too was crying, his eyes burning from the smoke and the tears.

*

They found a phone box at a beach north of the port, and then showered, the bright sodium lights of the cranes glowing across the silky black ocean. It was warm and still, but Emma shivered as Lee dried her with the blanket from the van. She put her arms around him, and they whispered to one another.

When Emma's father's red Volvo pulled into the parking lot, Lee watched from a distance: Emma standing alone under a streetlight, moths batting above her head, the Volvo spearing across the broad spaces of the empty lot and skidding alongside her.

Her father was wearing a suit, and he nearly fell over in his rush. He grabbed her and held her close as she lay her head on his shoulder.

26.

It was dark in the karri forest, the pale trunks rising to the canopy swooshing in the wind. Lee had taken back roads south along the coast and the van was coated with a red dust, bugs sprayed across the edges of the windshield where the wipers couldn't reach. He stopped in the middle of the forest on a hard shoulder covered in bark rinds and bought a twenty-kilo bag of apples from an honesty stall, leaving the five dollar note under a brick inside an iron cage.

As soon as he left the forest, the sky opened and the soil turned sandy grey. A farmer had drawn him a mud map on the back of a tourist brochure, and he slowed and saw the hand-painted sign beside another dirt track and took a bite of an apple and turned onto the track.

He didn't have any idea which direction he was headed, but soon the spaces between the low trees began to widen. Balga trees and ti-tree began to clump together, and he could smell briny water, and the sandy track became pale and he knew that he was near an estuary of some sort.

He glanced at the mud map as he drove, the van's wheels skidding in the turns, a flock of black cockatoos rising in a cawing wave to circle above him, a family of kangaroos hopping onto the edges of the track and watching him pass. He knew that he was close and slowed, smelled the smoke on the wind, heard a windmill blade turn through its circle.

The track thinned out and then he was driving on pea-gravel and his wheels were loud in it and he saw the farmhouse up ahead. The sun shone on a spray of water from a hose fixed to a star picket and he looked at the scarecrow next to it dressed in faded dungarees and gumboots and a big floppy hat, and then the scarecrow moved, and turned into a woman. She raised a hand to shield her eyes from the sun, just as a kelpie pup joined her, standing with its ears cocked and tail aloft.

Lee kept driving. He knew that the road would lead to an estuary and a river mouth, the coastal dunes where he'd make camp, set himself up with a tarp and a blanket, a jerry can of water and his remaining Rohypnol, to get himself clean and wear the suffering due to him. He didn't want his mother to see him sick. He looked at her in his rear-vision, her hand still cocked to her head, shielding her eyes from the glare, watching the van disappear into its coiling tail of dust.

AUTHOR NOTE

True West is set in late 1980s Perth against the backdrop of hate crimes associated with Jack van Tongeren's Australian Nationalist Movement that included the firebombing of Asian businesses, as well as the dog-whistle comments made by then federal Liberal opposition leader John Howard associated with 'slowing down' Asian immigration. It's fair to say that the men of the ANM were socially marginal figures and yet it's also true to say that because of their propaganda, and their actions, this period wasn't a comfortable time to be an Asian-Australian in Perth. Van Tongeren was ultimately sentenced to thirteen years imprisonment for his crimes, while John Howard went on to become one of Australia's longest serving prime ministers. This historical Conservative integration with and curtailing of the extreme right by accommodating anti-Asian and, more recently, anti-Muslim rhetoric is neither durable nor without danger. It cannot be denied that the recent expression of openly racist sentiments in the Australian parliament, for example, contribute to perpetrators' justification for horrific acts of violence, such as those that occurred in Christchurch in March 2019. *True West* is, however, entirely a work of fiction, and any resemblance to real people living or dead is coincidental.

At p.116, I have included a quote within from Friedrich Nietzsche's *Thus Spake Zarathustra* (1883–1891). And at p.55, Lee paraphrases Michael Bakunin, from *Michael Bakunin: Selected Writings* (Grove Press, 1974).

I owe a deal of gratitude to my first readers – Mark Constable, Sean Gorman, Rob Schofield and Andrew Nette – whose advice was invaluable in improving the rough early draft. This novel is dedicated to author and pulp scholar Andrew Nette for his friendship and encouragement, for deepening my knowledge of the genre and making me want to be a better writer. I've long admired Andrew's writing and his advocating for darker-edged Australian crime writing. Thanks always to my publisher and editor, Georgia Richter, for seeing what this novel might become and gently guiding me there, as well as to my publicist Claire Miller and all the team at Fremantle Press. Love and thanks always to my family – Belinda, Max, Fairlie and Luka.

Trainee private investigator Lee Southern finds himself drawn into a web of danger and deceit as he investigates a series of bribery attempts targeting a wealthy entrepreneur. Under the expert tutelage of retiring PI Frank Swann, Lee uses all of his developing skills, instincts and cunning to get to the heart of a sordid mystery. As Lee delves deeper into the case and questions the intentions of those he's working for, he finds himself the target of increasingly ominous threats and several attempts on his life.

David Whish-Wilson's *I Am Already Dead* is a gripping and high-paced noir novel. This will keep fans of True West on the edge of their seat.

AVAILABLE AT FREMANTLEPRESS.COM.AU

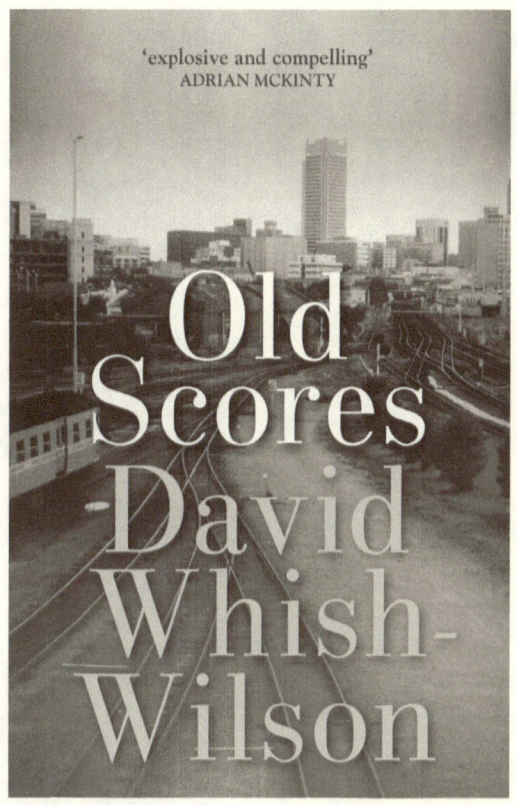

MORE GREAT CRIME

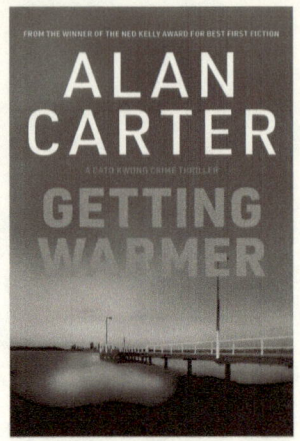

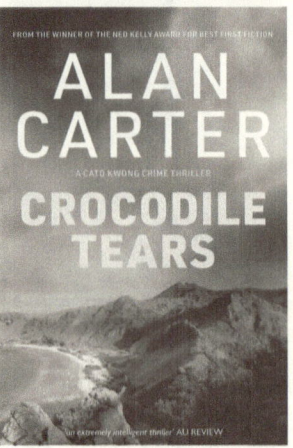

 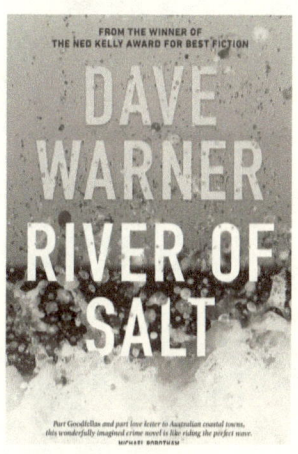

First published 2019 by
FREMANTLE PRESS

Fremantle Press Inc. trading as Fremantle Press
PO Box 158, North Fremantle, Western Australia, 6159
fremantlepress.com.au

Cover photograph by Tim Robinson © Arcangel Images
Designed by Nada Backovic, nadabackovic.com

 A catalogue record for this
book is available from the
National Library of Australia

ISBN 9781925815702 (paperback)
ISBN 9781925815719 (ebook)

Fremantle Press is supported by the Western Australian State
Government through the Department of Cultural Industries, Tourism
and Sport.

Fremantle Press respectfully acknowledges the Whadjuk people of the
Noongar nation as the Traditional Owners and Custodians of the land
where we work in Walyalup.

www.ingramcontent.com/pod-product-compliance
Lightning Source LLC
Chambersburg PA
CBHW030645030726
47497CB00006B/1954